JAILED, BAILED AND TAILED

"Do the people behind us belong to you?" Dee asked.

With some difficulty Lando managed to swivel around and look out the back window. There was a large hover truck right behind them. Dee changed lanes and the truck followed.

"I don't think so," Lando replied. "My people would follow in a taxi or something like that."

"I was afraid of that," the red-haired bounty hunter said grimly. "How 'bout that chrome-plated cyborg you waxed on Dista? Is there any chance he's after you?"

Lando thought about Jord Willer. "Yeah, he's a distinct possibility, although I can't see how he'd find me here."

"You've got to be kidding." Dee hit the gas and screeched around a corner.

Lando looked up just in time to see another set of headlights coming straight at them. There was no place to go. Dee stood on the brakes and pulled her gun at the same time. "Keep your head down, Lando. It's worth a lot of money."

"Well-paced . . . original . . . read this one just for fun. You won't regret it."
— *Isaac . . . . Fiction Magazine*

"A straightforwa **action!"**

D1041252

DRIFTER'S RUN

WILLIAM C. DIETZ

ACE BOOKS, NEW YORK

This book is an Ace original edition,
and has never been previously published.

DRIFTER'S RUN

An Ace Book / published by arrangement with
the author

PRINTING HISTORY
Ace edition / June 1992

ISBN: 0-441-16814-0

Ace Books are published by The Berkley Publishing Group,
200 Madison Avenue, New York, New York 10016.
The name "ACE" and the "A" logo
are trademarks belonging to Charter Communications, Inc.

PRINTED IN THE UNITED STATES OF AMERICA

10 9 8 7 6 5 4 3 2 1

This book is for Allison and Jessica,
who taught me everything I know about
little girls, and who make it a pleasure
to come home every day.

1

Lando looked up from his bowl of stew and swore softly. A cylindrical robo-laser had appeared over his table. Its antigrav unit hummed ominously while a ruby-red eye regarded him with mechanical malevolence. Lando resisted the impulse to run. That was the robo-laser's purpose, to pin him down, to keep him in place. If he moved more than a foot in any direction, the tubular device would send a spear of bright blue energy straight through his brain.

Using slow, deliberate movements Lando spooned more stew into his mouth. Which one of them was after him? The spacer in black leather? The overdressed pimp? The mercenary with the burned face?

The Roid Miner's Rest was packed with people. They filled the place to overflowing, talking, laughing, smoking, enjoying a brief moment of relaxation in otherwise dangerous lives. They were dressed like what they were, spacers on a half-rotation shore leave, miners just in from the asteroid belt, prostitutes both male and female, looking for tricks.

But somewhere among them was a bounty hunter, one of the countless thousands who made a living picking the empire's lice from its ratty fur, men and women often no better than the vermin they sought.

The empire's taxpayers viewed bounty hunters as a low-cost alternative to an interstellar police force, but like all the rest of the criminals they hunted, Lando saw them as human vultures feeding off the less fortunate.

As Lando looked at the crowd they looked back. The robo-laser meant trouble, *his* trouble, and they were curious.

What they saw was a slim young man in his late twenties.

Lando wore a good quality one-piece ship-suit with lots of pockets and zippers. His shiny black hair was pulled into a short ponytail in back. He had quick brown eyes, a hooked nose, and a thin-lipped mouth that smiled as the crowd grew silent.

"Which one of you belongs to this worthless piece of junk?" Lando asked, gesturing up toward the robo-laser.

The crowd stirred as a man stepped forward. He was small, almost tiny, and extremely dapper. His clothes were fancy, the kind gamblers wear, and his boots had a ten-credit shine. He brought his nerve lash up in a casual salute.

"The device in question belongs to me, sir . . . and I'll thank you to show a little more respect. It's worth more than the price on your head."

Lando shook his head sadly. "I'm sorry to hear that. Allow me to offer my condolences regarding its loss."

The movement of Lando's wrist was almost too quick to follow but the results were impossible to miss. The tiny heat-seeking micro-missile barely had time to arm itself before it struck the robo-laser and blew up.

The crowd scattered as pieces of red-hot metal and plastic fell on their heads. Lando stood, hoping to escape during the confusion, but found himself looking down the barrel of a huge slug gun. Where the hell did that come from? Lando dived for the floor.

The bounty hunter's gun made a loud booming noise as a high-velocity slug whipped through the space that Lando's head had occupied only moments before.

Lando rolled as he hit the floor and scrabbled for his slug thrower. It took what seemed like an eternity to pull the pistol free, line it up with the bounty hunter's chest, and squeeze the trigger. The sharp cracking sound seemed like an afterthought.

The slug hit the bounty hunter in the center of his chest and threw him backward into a post. But rather than slide toward the floor as he should, the bounty hunter staggered and recovered his balance.

Armor! The miserable bastard wore body armor!

Lando rolled left as two more slugs thumped into the floor where he'd been. Damn! This was getting serious.

Some chairs got in his way and Lando did the only thing

he could. His right arm jerked as another micro-missile raced away, this one hitting the ceiling with a sharp crack and filling the room with smoke.

So much for the missile launcher. Now Lando was down to the slug gun and a small blaster in his right boot.

Coughing and hacking on the noxious smoke, Lando was halfway to the rear exit when the nerve lash came down across the top of his shoulders. The little bastard wouldn't give up!

Incredible pain lanced down through Lando's muscles causing him to stagger and fall. He hit hard, rolled, and fired up through the smoke.

The bounty hunter dropped the nerve lash in order to grab his right thigh. It pumped bright red blood and collapsed under his weight.

Lando struggled to his feet. He aimed the slug gun at the bounty hunter's head. By all rights he should kill the bastard. He couldn't do it . . . not in cold blood anyway. Lando backed up until he felt the wall. He slid along it toward the door. The crowd. He had to watch the crowd. Maybe the bounty hunter had a partner, a friend, or another robo-laser. The bounty hunter moaned and rolled back and forth.

Nobody tried to help him. Lando felt the door and backed through it.

It took him two minutes to run up a narrow flight of metal stairs and go out through the saloon's emergency air lock. Lando found himself in a narrow access way with nothing but a maze of pipes and ducts overhead and metal walls to either side. There was a slice of light at the far end of the passage. He headed that way.

Seconds later Lando stepped out into a filthy tube way and heard the whoop of distant sirens. Time to get a move on.

The local police would ignore whatever crimes he'd committed elsewhere but they'd see him as a troublemaker and throw him in jail for disturbing the peace. Lando would prove self-defense, but that would take days, and he was in a hurry. Besides, Lando's motto was "go with the flow," and how can you "go with the flow" if you're in jail?

Forcing himself to ignore the pain, Lando became someone else. A power tech just off his ship out to see the sights. Both sides of the tube way were packed with stores, saloons, and brothels.

Lights flashed, music blared, and robo-hawkers dashed here and there vying for customers.

Lando waved at the police car when it rolled by and grinned when the cops ignored him. It brought back memories of his father.

"Never run, boy, always walk. Guilty people run. Smile, wave at people you don't know, try to fit in. That's the way to keep your ass outta the slammer, son."

And like most of his father's advice it worked. Ten minutes after leaving the Roid Miner's Rest, Lando was six grids down the tube way, and in the midst of the cheaper flophouses. His was one of the worst.

Styling itself as the "Economy Hotel," it was nothing more than a pile of fifty 8-by-4 shipping modules, stacked five high, and open at one end. About ten years ago someone had thrown a pallet into each module. That, plus a ragged curtain, comprised each room's decor.

The lobby was nothing more than the section of tube way that happened to be adjacent to the owner's beat-up metal desk. The owner's name was Mabe, not for "Mabel," but for "maybe." She more than filled the standard shuttle seat behind the desk. As usual, Mabe was busy chewing someone out for an offense fancied or real. The culprit, or victim as the case may be, was a wimpy little guy. He stood with head hung low.

Lando paused a few doors down and scanned the area for signs of trouble.

Had the bounty hunter followed him to the Roid Miner's Rest? Or spotted him and acted on impulse? What if the bounty hunter had a partner? If so the hotel could be a trap waiting to be sprung.

Lando spent the next fifteen minutes looking for a trap but didn't see one. Putting a spring in his step and a smile on his face, Lando approached Mabe's desk.

Mabe scowled. She had gimlet eyes set in a doughy face and surrounded by a halo of short, greasy hair.

"So what's this? Back a bit early ain't ya? Don't tell me ya ran outta credits. Well, no problem. I'll sell your duffel, and bingo, we're even."

"Thanks for the generous offer," Lando said dryly, "but if it's all the same to you I'll pay my bill in the usual way."

Mabe shrugged massive shoulders. "Jus tryin' ta help, darlin', jus tryin' ta help. Two cycles plus storage comes ta a hundred even."

The price was outrageous, but so was everything else, and Lando had no choice but to pay. An altercation with Mabe, a call to the police, and they'd take him away. His description was all over moon base by now.

Smiling, Lando pulled two fifties out of a breast pocket, and threw them on Mabe's desk. He knew without looking that he had about twenty left. "I'll take my bag now."

After checking the currency under a beat-up scanner, Mabe got to her feet and waddled over to a large metal trunk. Lando heard a distinct click as the woman placed a pudgy thumb against the print-lock and the squeal of unoiled hinges as she lifted the lid.

At that point Lando was treated to the sight of Mabe's enormous bottom as she bent over and reached inside the trunk. He feared it would give him nightmares for days to come.

Mabe straightened, wiped her nose with the back of her hand, and turned around. Lando's black duffel bag made a soft thump as it hit the top of her desk.

It was an expensive bag, with a pick-proof lock, and a rather ingenious secret compartment. A compartment equipped with some very expensive electronics, electronics designed to make it seem as though the compartment wasn't there.

Just part of a smuggler's kit and all that Lando had left. The nice clothes, fat bank account, and fast ship were all things of the past. Left behind when he fled Ithro.

"Thanks, Mabe," Lando said lightly. "You run a class act. Keep up the good work."

Mabe watched Lando's suitcase until it faded into the crowd. Then she sighed and turned back to her desk. It was too bad. The suitcase had caught her fancy. Ah, well. According to Mabe's most recent calculations, she could retire in another five years, seven months, and three days. Then she'd buy whatever kind of suitcase she wanted, load it with cash, and blast off this godforsaken pus ball. Mabe sighed, and looked around for someone to abuse.

The pain in Lando's back had died down to a dull aching throb. He needed some painkiller, food to replace the stew he didn't get to eat, and a job. Seeing a public terminal up ahead,

Lando decided he'd tackle the last problem first.

After waiting while a miner checked the latest price for aluminum, Lando stepped up to the terminal and scanned the main menu.

There it was in alphabetical order, the word "Employment," followed by "Encyclopedia." He chose "Employment."

As Lando touched the screen a new menu rolled up. It offered hundreds of possibilities, starting with "Accountant," and going on from there. Lando watched the job titles roll by until the word "Pilot" appeared on the screen. He speared it with a finger. It stopped and disappeared as data flooded the screen.

Like most smugglers, Lando could fly damned near anything, and had. Up till now he'd seen the skill as a means to an end, a useful adjunct to moving large amounts of tax-free merchandise from one place to another, but not as a job.

But what the hell, flying beat the hell out of scrubbing hydroponics tanks, and would help Lando put a few more lights between himself and the police on Ithro.

Enthusiasm quickly gave way to depression as Lando ran his eye down a short list of rather dismal possibilities. The good stuff never made it to the public terms. Nine times out of ten people hire people they already know.

Lando saw that he could fly a mail run into the asteroids, ride shotgun aboard a high G med-ship, or sign as third officer on a tramp freighter.

None of them looked very attractive. The mail run was a good way to get killed, the high G med-ship would probably take ten years off his life, and the tramp freighter was headed toward Ithro.

Lando was about to clear the screen and walk when a new entry appeared: "Pilot sought for deep-space tug. Competitive salary, plus a percentage of salvage, spacious cabin, and friendly crew. Humanoids preferred but not necessary. Dopers, missionaries, politicians, and space lawyers need not apply."

A time and place for interviews followed.

Seeing no specific prohibition against smugglers, Lando stabbed the button labeled "Print," and waited while a sheet of plastic fax whirred from the side of the terminal.

A tug wasn't Lando's idea of heaven, but it beat the heck out of the other three possibilities.

As Lando turned away a birdlike Finthian stepped in to take his place.

A close reading of the printout revealed that Lando had two hours to kill prior to the first scheduled interview. He used it to obtain a blister pak full of pain tabs, a sandwich filled with tasty vegetables, and a quick shower. It took five of his remaining credits but was worth it.

Showered, shaved, and dressed in his second ship-suit Lando felt and looked much better. "Show people what they want to see, son," his father had always said, "and they'll hear what you have to say."

It took a half hour to make the trip from the public showers to a middle-of-the-road hotel called the Starman's Inn, identify himself at the front desk, and drop to level four. According to the desk clerk Captain Sorenson occupied Suite 437.

Eyeing the doors, Lando watched the numbers get larger, 433, 435, and, yes, 437. As Lando approached, the door opened and a man stepped out.

He was tall, thin, and stooped over, as if years in small ships had somehow compressed him. There were no eyebrows over his bright blue eyes.

The man shook his head. "Don't waste your time, lad. You'd do better humping cargo or swabbing decks."

Lando had questions, lots of them, but by the time he had them ready the man was already halfway down the corridor and headed for the lift tubes.

Lando shrugged. Chances were the man was right, but what the heck, he could always say no.

Lando touched the door and heard a distant chime. "Come in!" The voice was faint and surprisingly childlike.

Lando pushed the door open and stepped inside. The suite was comfortable but not plush. The sort of quarters favored by traveling salesmen and tourists on a budget.

The walls were tuned to a pattern of rather amorphous blue bubbles that appeared from under the floor and floated slowly upward to disappear beyond the ceiling.

A thousand feet had worn a path toward a low arch and the bedroom beyond. The sitting room boasted a beat-up power lounge, a stained couch, and a small desk.

A little girl sat behind the desk and watched Lando with big solemn eyes.

He didn't know much about children, but Lando guessed the girl was nine or ten years old. She had brown-blond hair, an upturned nose, and a round face. She spoke with great care, like an actress reciting lines.

"Welcome. My name is Melissa Sorenson. Are you here to apply for the position of pilot?"

Lando nodded. "Yes. Is Captain Sorenson in?"

Melissa Sorenson bit her lip, seemed to realize it, and stopped.

"No, I'm afraid my father is sick right now, but I'd be happy to take your application. Would you care to sit down?"

Lando was starting to have real misgivings, but the little girl was so earnest, so serious, that he couldn't bring himself to walk out. It might hurt her feelings.

He sat on the power lounge. It groaned, creaked, and whined into an upright position.

"Now," the little girl said, consulting the portacomp in front of her, "I'd like to ask you some questions."

"Shoot," Lando replied, and mentally prepared himself for a play-pretend interview. No wonder the man left. This was absurd.

"Imagine that you are the pilot of a Hexon Class IV gas transport. You've just dropped out of hyperspace in the vicinity of a white dwarf. The NAVCOMP activates your standard drives but both drop off-line. Your board is green, the NAVCOMP claims everything's A-okay, and the chief engineer is completely mystified. What do you do?"

Lando was only a few words into his answer when he began to sweat. The question seemed simple enough, but in order to answer it, he'd have to demonstrate a working knowledge of that particular make of ship, the drives it had, and the standard diagnostic procedures for a green-board power failure.

Since the board was green, and the chief engineer was mystified, chances were that the NAVCOMP had malfunctioned and the drives were okay. But there were other possibilities too, and in order to provide the little girl with a complete answer, Lando would be forced to deal with those as well.

It took Lando fifteen minutes to answer the first question. The second, third, fourth, and fifth took even longer, as did the sixth, seventh, eighth, and ninth.

By the time Lando had finished the tenth question he'd been

in Suite 437 for more than three hours. He was exhausted and Melissa Sorenson was fresh as a daisy. Not only that, but Lando was fairly sure that she'd understood all of his answers, and found some of them inadequate.

Whatever Melissa's reaction she typed it into the portacomp with more than average skill. After a minute or two the girl stopped typing and looked up. "Your name?"

For a moment Lando debated the merits of using his name versus an alias. In the technical sense he was wanted on Ithro, and only Ithro, although bounty hunters could follow him anywhere.

So, it probably made sense to use another name, but there was something about Melissa's trusting eyes that made it hard to lie. "My name's Pik Lando."

Melissa nodded, typed the information into her portacomp, and asked a routine series of questions. World of origin, next of kin, and so forth. For the most part Lando told the truth.

When she was done the girl straightened up as if to make herself bigger. "When can you start?"

Lando raised his eyebrows in surprise. "You're making me an offer?"

The girl was suddenly crestfallen. Her lower lip began to tremble. "You don't want the job?"

Suddenly on the defensive, Lando held up a hand. "No, no, I didn't say that. I just wondered if you should consult with your father or something."

All signs of concern vanished from Melissa's face. "Oh, no, Daddy always goes along with my decisions, he calls me his little business agent." She smiled brightly.

Lando sighed. Great. A deep-space tug with a ten-year-old girl as its business agent. On the other hand, anything that made him hard to find was a plus right now, and a tug could be just the ticket.

He forced a smile. "I see. Tell me, Ms. Sorenson . . ."

"Everyone calls me Melissa. Except Daddy that is. He calls me Mel."

"Thanks. My friends call me Pik. Tell me, Melissa, if I accept the job, where's the ship headed?"

The girl looked thoughtful. "That's hard to say, Pik. Daddy works this system mostly, but we'll go anywhere if the price is right, and the big companies let us. Daddy will find something. He always does."

Lando nodded understandingly. Well, what the hell. Anywhere was better than here. And even if it wasn't he could always quit, and go to work for someone else.

He smiled. "Okay, Melissa, you've got yourself a pilot. And in answer to your original question, I can start right now."

Melissa's face lit up with happiness. "Really? That's wonderful, Pik. Now, if you'll thumbprint this contract, we'll be all set."

Suddenly Lando found himself holding a neat-looking printout, six pages of printout to be exact, single-spaced and full of legal jargon.

Skimming through the contract, Lando saw all the usual responsibility, liability, and damage clauses, along with two other paragraphs of special interest.

One granted him a slightly substandard salary, with the promise of a "ten percent share of any salvage that said company might realize during the lifetime of the contract," and the other obligated him to "Sorenson Tug & Salvage for a minimum of six standard months, or until injury, dismemberment, or death renders the incumbent unable to carry out his/her duties."

The wording seemed slightly redundant but Lando got the idea. It was a good contract, good for Sorenson Tug & Salvage that is, and it caused Lando to eye Melissa suspiciously.

But her cute little face was absolutely free from any hint of guile, sharp dealing, or subterfuge. For one fleeting moment Lando considered asking for more money, but it didn't seem fair to lean on a ten-year-old girl, so he let it go.

Lando signed by pressing his thumb against the lower right-hand corner of the contract, accepted his copy, and watched the original disappear into a small case along with Melissa's portacomp.

The girl was organized, you had to give her that.

Melissa looked up and smiled. "Do you need to collect your gear or something?"

"Nope," Lando replied, "everything I need is all right there." He gestured toward the suitcase that he'd left by the door.

An adult might have questioned the single bag, or the fact that Lando had it with him, but not Melissa.

Like most children she took adult activities at face value, unless they had something to do with business, in which case Melissa assumed they were lying. Except for the ones who underestimated her abilities ... and they deserved whatever they got.

Melissa moved on to the next problem. "Good. In that case I'll call for a robo-porter."

"A robo-porter?" Lando asked, looking around the room. "What for? Have you got lots of luggage or something?"

Melissa giggled. "Heavens no! I travel light. It's for Daddy. The spaceport's quite a ways from here ... and Daddy's too heavy for me to carry."

"Too heavy for you to carry ..." Lando said suspiciously. "What's wrong with him? Where is he?"

Melissa put a finger to her lips and motioned for Lando to follow. Together they tiptoed into the bedroom. The walls were dimmed to near darkness but Lando had no difficulty seeing a man sprawled across the bed.

Moving in closer, Melissa patted the man's shoulder protectively and looked up into Lando's face. There was something sad about her expression.

"This is my daddy. He's sick, but he'll wake up in two or three hours."

Lando felt a sinking feeling in the pit of his stomach as his eyes confirmed what his nose already told him. Melissa's father, Captain Ted Sorenson, wasn't sick. Not in the usual sense anyway. He was dead drunk.

2

It took more than two hours to load Captain Sorenson's unconscious form aboard the robo-porter, cover it with a blanket, and make their way up to the moon's surface.

Lando had expected a certain amount of attention. After all, the combination of a man, a little girl, and what appeared to be a dead body should turn a few heads, and would have anywhere else.

But most of those who lived in the moon station saw stranger sights every day, and besides, they had other things to worry about. Like making enough credits to go somewhere else.

The robo-porter was little more than a beat-up metal platform with a drive mechanism and a low order processor. Having accepted a load, the robo-porter would electronically imprint on its customer, and follow until released.

Nice in theory, but their particular machine had some sort of processing dysfunction, and followed anyone of Lando's approximate size and shape. As a result it had a tiresome tendency to carry its unconscious passenger off in unpredictable directions.

Each time they chased the robo-porter down Lando was forced to stand in front of the machine, recycle its imprint function, and start all over. That, plus a screeching drive wheel, was just about to drive Lando crazy when Melissa found a solution.

The robo-porter had just followed a tall willowy naval lieutenant down a side corridor, when Melissa called, "Hey, Pik! Wait a minute! I think I've got the answer."

Taking Lando's place in front of the robo-porter's eye, Melissa recycled the imprint function, and led the device away. Ten minutes and a whole series of twists and turns later, the machine was still with them.

"It's 'cause I'm smaller," Melissa explained cheerfully. "There aren't very many kids around here, so there's less chance of a screwup."

About fifteen minutes later they left a lift tube and entered a large open space. A transparent dome curved up and over their heads. The planet Snowball hung suspended above them. It seemed ready to fall at any moment.

Lando assured himself that it wouldn't happen. And given the laws of physics, the moon wouldn't fall on Snowball either.

The planet had a slightly pink albedo and a surface temperature of −290 degrees F.

The atmosphere was too thick to see through, but Lando knew most of the planet's surface was covered with oceans of ethane, ebbing and flowing around occasional islands of ice.

Just great for the robotic gas scoops that cruised the planet's surface but not very good for people. They stayed on the moon.

The dome's floor was part passenger terminal and part warehouse. All sorts of sentients came and went. Lando saw humans, Finthians, Zords, Lakorians, and a few aliens he couldn't name, all going about their various chores.

Meanwhile hundreds of machines rolled, whirred, hissed, rumbled, and creaked their way through the crowd.

There were lowboys stacked high with cargo modules, tall mincing auto loaders stepping over and around sentients and machines alike, and short multi-armed maintenance bots that dashed every which way in a valiant attempt to keep things running.

Working together the sentients and their machine helpers were trying to load, unload, and service the circle of ships that surrounded the dome.

There were freighters, couriers, scouts, tankers, and a dozen more. Appearance depended on function, racial preference, and a whole host of other factors. In fact, the only thing the ships had in common was their size. All of them were small. Due to the moon's gravity, and the relatively small dome, larger ships were forced to remain in orbit.

"Our tender's over there," Melissa said eagerly as she pointed across the dome. "Lock 78."

Now that negotiations were over Lando noticed that Melissa had undergone a change. The mostly serious business manager had disappeared. In her place was a naturally gregarious little girl. Of the two Lando preferred the second.

"It's a good thing you're here," Melissa said seriously, "Daddy gets mad when I fly the tender. He says I'm too young. Still, what am I supposed to do when he's sick?

"Mom flew the tender when she was alive, she could do anything, but that was a long time ago. She died trying to salvage a wreck. Daddy said it would have been a big score, big enough to retire on, but the wreck's drives went critical and blew up. I miss Mommy . . . but Daddy and I do okay. Do you have any children?"

An alcoholic father, a dead mother, Melissa's nine or ten years had been far from pleasant. Lando felt a tightness in his throat. "No, Melissa. I don't have any children. But if I did, I'd want a little girl just like you."

Melissa's eyes shone as she looked up into his face. "Really? You're probably just saying that to be nice, but I like it anyway. We're almost there."

The robo-porter picked that particular moment to follow a short, stumpy Lakorian toward a distant ship, but was quickly retrieved and guided to Lock 78.

Melissa touched the red indicator light located next to the lock and was rewarded with a synthesized voice. It said, "Manual override engaged. Please call for attendant."

Melissa said something ungirlish under her breath and hit the attendant call button.

It took a while, but eventually a Zord rolled up, stepped off his motorized platform, and examined them with a baleful eye. Like all of his race the Zord was vaguely humanoid. But while the alien had two legs, four armlike tentacles, and a skinny torso, any resemblance to a human ended there. Folds of brown leathery skin hung all over his face, and a writhing mass of tentacles surrounded his oral cavity.

Because Zords have no vocal apparatus they use the tentacles that surround their oral cavities to communicate via high-speed sign language.

While Lando knew enough sign language to get by, Melissa was a good deal more proficient, and took charge of the situation. Melissa's fingers were a blur of motion as she stated her case.

The tentacles around the Zord's mouth writhed in response, and although most of the interchange was too fast for Lando to follow, it was soon apparent that some sort of dispute was in progress.

It seemed that Melissa wanted to charge the docking fee to her father's account, and that was fine with the Zord so long as she paid the existing balance first.

Melissa replied that she'd be happy to pay the existing balance, if and when the station paid the damages owed her father from their last visit. She claimed that a deranged maintenance bot had entered the ship, dismantled part of the control system, and left.

At this point the Zord consulted his portacomp, found no records pertaining to a deranged maintenance bot, and noticed that an incoming shuttle was queued up for Melissa's slot.

On the universal theory that time is money, the Zord decided to let the matter of the unpaid balance go for the moment, and settled for a two-day docking fee cash-on-the-portacomp.

Melissa agreed, and as she produced exact change from a carefully zipped pocket, Lando got the feeling that things had gone her way. The smug little smile that she wore as the lock hissed open seemed to confirm it.

It took a while to maneuver the robo-porter through the tender's lock, down a short corridor, and into a tiny cabin.

After that they rolled Captain Sorenson into a bunk, strapped him in, and guided the robot out through the lock.

As the lock cycled closed Lando headed for the ship's control room. The tender was larger than Lando had expected, and a good deal newer, although he didn't see a scrap of luxury in her boxy hull. She looked like what she was, a good honest work boat, sturdy and plain.

Lando noticed that the ship was clean and well maintained. Good. At least Sorenson did *something* right.

The control room was small, but not especially cramped. As Lando dropped into the pilot's seat the tender's navigational computer sensed his presence and activated the ship's control panel.

"Welcome," a voice said. "Please provide appropriate identification."

Lando looked at Melissa. She smiled. "This is Melissa. Confirm."

A moment passed while the computer recorded her voice, analyzed it, and confirmed her identity. "Identity confirmed," the voice said. "Instructions?"

"Meet Pik Lando," Melissa replied. "He'll have level one access to this ship. Confirm."

"Level one access confirmed," the computer replied. "Recording."

"Say something," Melissa instructed, "so the NAVCOMP has a sample of your voice."

Lando thought for a moment and said:

> "Cannon to right of them,
> Cannon to left of them,
> Cannon in front of them
>   Volley'd and thunder'd
> Storm'd at with shot and shell,
> Boldly they rode and well,
> Into the jaws of death,
> Into the mouth of hell."

"Identity recorded," the computer said. "Thank you."

There was curiosity in Melissa's eyes. "What was that?"

"One of my father's favorite poems," Lando replied. "He was a soldier in his younger days and had a taste for blood and thunder poetry."

"Where's your father now?" Melissa asked, completely oblivious to the pain in Lando's eyes.

"He's dead," Lando replied gruffly, and for a moment he remembered the ambush, the hell of blaster fire, his father's charred body.

Well, the bastards had paid for their treachery, and paid in blood. For as his father fell, Lando had turned three men and the sand they stood on into black glass. He'd been on the run ever since.

Lando pushed the thoughts away and turned his attention

to the tender's control panel. As his fingers danced across the buttons, Lando missed Melissa's hurt look and the slight tremble in her lower lip.

Screens came to life, indicator lights shifted from amber to green, and a faint whine sounded inside the cabin. The tender was ready to lift.

Lando double-checked his indicator lights, got a clearance from moon station traffic control, and fired both drives. The ship lifted up and away.

"Lots of power," Lando commented, glancing in Melissa's direction.

The little girl had strapped herself into the co-pilot's position. Something about the way Melissa sat there told Lando that she really *could* fly the tender if she had to. It was clear she didn't want to though, and Melissa looked relieved as the tender moved up and away, a dot against Snowball's vast presence.

"Yup," Melissa said, patting the tender's control panel, "Daddy says she has strong legs. And hyperdrive too. Daddy says we're lucky to have her. Even though she isn't big enough for a serious tow, we can use her beams to move things around, and that helps a lot. We got her from a tramp freighter. They couldn't pay their bill, so Daddy took the tender in trade."

"He got a good deal," Lando said matter-of-factly. "Where's your ship?"

Melissa punched some instructions into the ship's computer and nodded her satisfaction when a three-dimensional representation of Snowball appeared on Lando's main control screen.

Because the tender was moving in the opposite direction, the moon was now in the process of disappearing behind Snowball's considerable bulk. A complex tracery of parking orbits had also appeared, each representing a ship, and each bearing an alphanumeric code.

"That's us," Melissa said, pointing to a red delta, with the code "J-14" flashing on and off next to it. The "J" stood for the first letter of the ship's name, and the "14" for the orbit to which that particular vessel was assigned.

"What's the 'J' stand for?" Lando asked as he put the tender into a long gentle curve. "Jasmine? Jennifer? Justine?"

"Of course not," Melissa said stoutly. "Those are silly names. 'J' stands for 'Junk.' "

"Junk?" Lando asked disbelievingly. "You have a tug named Junk?"

"Yes," Melissa said defensively. "And what's wrong with that? It's a joke. Mother was an engineer and a darned good one. Right after she married Daddy she designed *Junk* and put her together. Look! There she is!"

Melissa pointed toward a point of reflected light in the middle of the forward view screen. The point of light quickly resolved into a dark silhouette against the pink marbling of Snowball's surface.

Lando dumped power and fired the tender's retros. He gave the controls a gentle nudge and they slid along the tug's starboard side. Lando wanted a look at his new home.

In a few seconds Lando saw why Melissa's mother had christened the tug *Junk*. She was far from pretty. Larger spaceships rarely have the streamlined grace of smaller craft designed for atmospheric use, but they often have a symmetry that's pleasing to the eye, and a sense of majesty. Not this one. *Junk* was just plain ugly.

Most of her hull was cylindrical, a common enough shape, but that's where any similarity to other ships ended. For one thing the ship had two enormous drives fitted to her stern, understandable on a tug, but ugly as hell.

And adding insult to injury, *Junk* was equipped with heavy-duty lateral thrusters mounted bow and stern. Again, given the fact that tugs are often required to move heavy objects port and starboard, the thrusters made a lot of sense. Unfortunately however they looked like large black warts.

Then there was the bridge. On most ships it was nothing more than a control room tucked safely inside the vessel's hull. But *Junk*'s bridge looked a lot like its maritime forerunners. It was a long rectangular box mounted at right angles to the hull and perched atop two large pylons.

Lando guessed that the pylons were hollow and provided access to the rest of the ship. The purpose of the whole affair was clear, to provide good 360-degree visibility during close maneuvers, but like the rest of the ship's fittings the bridge helped give the ship a raw ungainly appearance.

And then there was the maze of weapons blisters, launch

tubes, cooling towers, com masts, solar panels, beam projectors, and God knows what else that covered the ship's hull like an exotic skin disease.

"Beautiful, isn't she?" Melissa asked, her face beaming as she watched the tug slide by.

"Just gorgeous," Lando agreed dryly, pulling up and firing retros to match speed with the tug. "Where's the launching bay?"

"Underneath the hull," Melissa replied, and pointed toward the deck.

Lando nodded and performed a full roll to the left. When the tender came out of the roll she was right under a rectangle of bright light and moving forward at the same speed as the larger ship.

"That was neat!" Melissa said enthusiastically. "Will you teach me to do that?"

"Sure, if it's okay with your father," Lando replied, watching the screens to make sure the tender was centered in the larger vessel's hatch. Once it was properly positioned Lando used the vessel's repulsors to move up and inside *Junk*'s sizable bay.

It was well lit and large enough to haul some freight. One end was full of neatly stacked equipment, porta thrusters, auxiliary beam generators, and other tools of the towing trade. None showed any tendency to drift away, which confirmed an artificial gravity unit somewhere on board. *Junk* wasn't pretty but she was well equipped.

Moving to the right Lando dropped the tender with a gentle thump.

A few minutes later air had been pumped in to replace vacuum and they were free to leave the tender. Melissa scurried toward the lock. "Whoa," Lando said gently. "If you want to be a pilot someday you've got some work to do."

Melissa looked confused and then her face cleared with sudden understanding. "Ooops! Sorry. 'The pilot is responsible for securing the ship's main power systems. These systems are automatic but shutdown should be verified.' " The words had a formal quality as if memorized from a manual.

Lando nodded. The next few minutes were spent powering down, running through a series of routine diagnostic programs, and making the ship secure.

When they were done Melissa looked at Lando questioningly, he nodded, and she rushed toward the lock. "Come on, Pik! I'll show you the ship!"

"What about your father?" Lando asked as he released his harness. "Shouldn't we move him out of the tender?"

"What for?" Melissa said pragmatically. "He's used to waking up in the tender."

"Terrific," Lando mumbled to himself as he made his way to the tender's lock, "the slob is used to waking up in the tender."

But Melissa didn't hear him because she was already outside the tender and skipping across the deck. As Lando stepped out of the lock and made his way down a short ladder he saw that someone had used some white hull paint to lay out a hopscotch diagram.

Though marred by a few repulsor burns the diagram was otherwise quite serviceable. Melissa was busy hopping and jumping her way through it.

Beyond her a tidy little speedster sat on shiny struts looking far too racy for *Junk*'s utilitarian launch bay. It reminded Lando of his own speedster, a Nister Needle, little more than a drive unit with a cockpit strapped on top. The perfect ship for a smuggler. Small, fast, and hard to detect. The speedster, like the ship that carried it, had been left behind on Ithro.

"What's the deal on the speedster?" Lando asked, nodding toward the little ship.

Melissa shrugged and stooped to pick up the burned-out memory chip she used as a marker. "About a year ago we found a wrecked yacht and took her in tow. There was no one on board so she was ours fair and square. We sold the hull but kept some of the stuff on board including the speedster. I think we should sell it and use the money to overhaul the hydroponics tank."

Melissa looked up and smiled. "Daddy says I'm right, but he likes to ride in the speedster once in a while, so nothing seems to happen."

Lando nodded. It fit the pattern. Captain Sorenson seemed to have a hard time seeing very far beyond his own needs.

"Come on!" Melissa said, taking Lando by the arm and pulling him along. "Let's find Cy. He'll want to meet you."

"Cy?" Lando inquired, allowing himself to be towed through

a lock and into the ship's interior. "Who's he?"

"Our engineer," Melissa replied happily. "And a good one too! Daddy says we're lucky to have him. Cy keeps everything up and running."

That's when a silvery ball appeared at the far end of the corridor and zoomed toward them. Lando threw himself against the wall and reached for his slug thrower. It was halfway out of its holster when Melissa grabbed his wrist. "Don't shoot! That's Cy!"

And just as Melissa spoke the silver ball came to a stop, hovered in front of them, and extruded a second vid pickup. Lando didn't know for sure but assumed the globe was equipped with some sort of fancy antigrav unit. "Hi, Mel. Who's this?"

"Our new pilot," Melissa answered seriously. "His name is Pik Lando. Pik, this is Cy Borg, our chief engineer."

"Their *only* engineer," Cy replied cheerfully, "but what the heck, with me around one is enough." There was a soft whirring noise and an articulated arm appeared.

Much to his amazement Lando found himself reaching out to shake with a three-fingered metal hand. It was cold and very strong.

"It's a pleasure, Cy. I hope you'll forgive my reaction. I had a run-in with an airborne robo-laser not long ago. It tried to slice, dice, and cook me for dinner."

"Perfectly understandable," the silver globe said reassuringly. "Happens all the time. I'm used to it."

"Cy had a body once," Melissa said soberly, "but he gambled it away."

The metal sphere bobbed up and down in apparent agreement. "That's right . . . and the moral is?"

"Don't gamble," Melissa replied automatically, "no matter what anyone says."

"That's right," Cy said approvingly. "Being a brain in a box has some advantages . . . but not many." The cyborg spun toward Lando. "I sometimes wonder who's got the rest of me . . . and how they're doing."

It was meant as a joke but Lando didn't laugh. Like most smugglers he'd spent a good deal of time in sleazy dives, rim-world saloons, and smoke-filled gambling dens. In some of them you could lose all your money, sell an arm or a leg, and keep on going. There was a good market for bio parts, and while most settled for one or two replaceable organs, some went all the way.

Those who did ended up as brains floating in a bath of nutrient liquid. For such as those there was little choice, a life of total isolation within themselves, or continued existence as a cyborg. Most became cyborgs.

Cyborgs came in all sorts of shapes and sizes, their forms frequently following function, and such was apparently the case with Cy. Though why he'd chosen to call himself Cy Borg, Lando couldn't imagine. Whatever the reason it didn't seem polite to ask.

"So how long have you been with the ship, Cy?" Lando inquired. "I notice that she's in pretty good shape for a . . ." he almost said, "pile of junk," but looked at Melissa and thought better of it. "For a tug," Lando finished lamely.

If Cy noticed, there was no sign of it in his cheerful response. "Well, thanks, Pik. I do my best. I guess I've been with Cap and Mel for a couple years now, ever since I ran into a little trouble on Joyo's Roid. She's a good ship, and now that we've got a pilot, I'll feel a whole lot better."

The cyborg turned in Melissa's direction. "Where's your father? Sick again?"

Melissa nodded. "You know how it is, Cy, I tried to stop him but he wouldn't listen."

"That's okay," the metal sphere replied. "It's not your fault, Mel. You hear me? It's not your fault."

"Sure, I hear you," Melissa replied easily. "It's not my fault. Hey, you wanta race me to the end of the corridor?"

"Not right now, honey," Cy replied. "I've gotta repair the number four pressor housing before we break orbit. You know how your father is when he wakes up. 'All hands man your stations!' and that sort of stuff."

Cy's vid pickup turned toward Lando. "Nice meeting you, Pik, welcome aboard, and let me know if there's anything I can do to help." And with that the cyborg used a jet of compressed air to squirt himself down the corridor.

"Wanta race?" Melissa inquired, and took off toward the opposite end of the corridor without waiting for Lando's response.

The smuggler followed along behind, marveling at her youthful exuberance, and wondering what he'd gotten himself into. First a ten-year-old business agent, then an alcoholic captain, and now a bodiless chief engineer. What next?

That's when the whoop of the ship's collision alarm sent Lando racing for the bridge.

3

Heart pounding and pulse racing Lando ran toward the lift tube. His boots made a thumping sound as they hit the metal deck and squares of light flashed by overhead. He caught up with and passed Melissa.

Now the whoop of the collision alarm was overlaid by a stern-sounding male voice. "This ship is in imminent danger of collision. I repeat, this ship is in imminent danger of collision. Evasive action *is* required. I repeat, evasive action *is* required. The pilot or another responsible officer should report to the bridge. I repeat, the pilot or another responsible officer should report to the bridge."

Lando skidded to a stop in front of a lift tube, slammed his hand against the white sensor plate, and jumped inside as a door hissed open. Eyes searched desperately for the emergency UP button. He found the red square, stabbed it with a stiff finger, and watched the door slide closed on Melissa's frightened face.

The platform rose so quickly that Lando's knees buckled and his stomach felt as if it were being shoved down through the deck. A chime sounded as the platform came to a stop and the door hissed open.

A bright green sign said "Control Room" and pointed to the right. As Lando left the lift tube and sprinted toward the center of the ship, he remembered the two pylons that connected the bridge to the vessel's hull. He'd come up through the center of the port pylon. There's nothing like learning your way around in the middle of a collision, Lando thought grimly.

The control area was up ahead, a softly lit curvature of green, amber, and red lights, topped by a semicircular screen. The screen showed ten or twelve distinctly different pictures. Each one represented a vid-cam eye view of surrounding space. Five or six showed all or part of Snowball.

But Lando didn't need the vid screens. The front, top, and sides of the bridge were entirely transparent. As a result he could see the problem with his naked eye. A vast darkness was inserting itself between *Junk* and Durna's sun. There was no mistaking the thing's silhouette. It was a ship, a big one, and damned close.

As Lando dropped into the pilot's seat, he estimated the other ship was only one, maybe two hundred yards away and moving closer.

There wasn't time to sequence the main drives. He decided to steal as much power as he could from the tiny fusion plant that ran the ship's environmental systems and feed it to the huge thrusters mounted along the starboard side. If he acted fast enough they might do the trick.

Lando's fingers danced over the keys, redirected power to the lateral thrusters, and fired them. Nothing. Only a display that read "Provide voice sample to activate manual override."

"Damn!" He was locked out of the control system!

Meanwhile the collision alarm continued to whoop its warning and the computerized voice continued to order people around.

But it was too late for that now. The other ship had blocked the sun and left only a nimbus of yellow light around its gigantic form. As it came closer Lando saw the name *Hercules* spelled out across its bow in green letters fifteen feet high. They flashed on and off like an advertisement for a ten-credit pleasure dome.

And then, just when a collision seemed inevitable, and a scream had formed in Lando's throat, the other ship veered away. Moments later it was gone, leaving Lando's pulse pounding in his head, and the taste of bile in the back of his throat.

Seconds later the collision alarm shut itself off and the synthesized voice stopped in midsentence. Lando was still in shock when a voice came from behind.

"Who the hell are you? And what're you doing on my ship?"

Lando swiveled his chair around and found himself face-to-face with Captain Ted Sorenson. He had bushy eyebrows, a long straight nose, and a tight thin-lipped mouth. His eyes were bright blue and nearly buried in deep cavernous sockets.

The rest was tall and thin. An alcoholic's body, starved for nutrients and forced to expend large amounts of energy countering the poison that Sorenson pumped into it.

"My name's Pik Lando," the smuggler replied, getting to his feet, "and I was *trying* to save your ship."

"I hired him, Daddy," Melissa said desperately, stepping in from the side to tug at her father's arm. "You were sick, and Pik brought you back."

Sorenson looked down at his daughter and his face underwent a sudden transformation. Hard lines turned soft, wrinkles disappeared, and his mouth turned upward in a smile. "You hired him? Well, good for you, honey. I can always count on my little business agent."

Melissa glowed as her father stepped up to offer Lando his hand. His words were civil, but his eyes were stone-hard and formed a barricade between him and the universe.

"Sorry, Lando, but that alarm scared hell out of me. What was it? A systems malfunction?" The captain's handshake was brisk and firm.

"Nope," Lando replied evenly. "It was a ship, a big one, and damned close. It had the name *Hercules* printed across the port bow in letters fifteen feet high. I tried to move *Junk* out of the way but was locked out."

Lando saw the other man's eyes narrow as if the name had some special meaning. "*Hercules* you say? You're sure of that?"

"Yes. Why? Do you know her?"

The other man shrugged thoughtfully. "Sure . . . everyone knows her. She belongs to Stellar Tug & Salvage. They like to give their tugs ancient 'H' names. You know, *Hercules, Hebe, Hecuba,* that sort of thing."

"I see," Lando replied thoughtfully. "Looking back, the whole thing seems deliberate, as if they came that close to scare us or something. Is this Stellar Tug & Salvage outfit known for things like that?"

"You bet they are," Melissa answered grimly. "They harass all the smaller operators. They want Daddy to quit, but he won't."

The worshipful way in which Melissa looked up into her father's face made Lando realize that she'd made the transformation from adult back to little girl.

Sorenson chuckled. "I'm not the hero my daughter makes me out to be. I'd cave in right now if I could afford to. But I can't, *Junk*'s all we've got so we tough it out. Let's see what they have to say. Now that I'm here the controls should respond."

Turning, Lando saw a message waiting light was blinking on and off. He touched it and watched as a com screen swirled to life. What he saw took some getting used to.

It was a cyborg. Not a sphere like Cy, but a huge thing with a human head and a chrome body. The com screen cut the cyborg off at the waist, but Lando saw that its upper torso had been carefully sculpted into a work of art. A representation of the male form so extreme it verged on parody.

As the cyborg moved its skin bulged with synthetic muscle, rippled over metallic bone, and shimmered with false life. Each rib was carefully defined, each muscle given its correct and proper size, each limb perfectly proportioned. The whole thing was a work of art, a living sculpture celebrating something lost, a terrible and endless sorrow.

It smiled and a shiver ran down Lando's spine. There was something frightening about the blond hair, the Adonis-like face, the perfectly modulated voice.

"Greetings, Captain Sorenson. I tried to speak with you face-to-face, but since you were undoubtedly drunk, this will have to do. You don't recognize me . . . but you may remember my name. It's Jord Willer, once second officer aboard the *Star of Empire,* and now captain of the tug *Hercules.*

"It's been a long time since we dropped out of hyperspace into the middle of Durna's asteroid belt, hasn't it? Of course it probably seems longer to me, since I spent so much of it in hospitals.

"But there I go, talking about myself when you're so much more interesting! In fact you're something of a legend around here, aren't you? The crazy old man who looks for the ship that isn't there. Well, guess what? I believe it's there, and when you find it, I'll be by to collect my share." And with that the com screen faded to black.

Turning, Lando saw that Sorenson's face had turned ashen gray, as if his life force had suddenly drained away. When Sorenson spoke his voice was little more than a croak.

"There's a load of robotic mining gear waiting in Orbit Level 4. Mel knows what to do. I'll be in my cabin." And he walked away.

Lando watched Sorenson go with a certain amount of misgiving. What was this stuff about dropping out of hyperspace into the middle of Durna's asteroid belt? And Cap being drunk? And this guy named Willer spending years in the hospital? Holy Sol, if Willer's injuries were Sorenson's fault, then no wonder the cyborg was pissed! Pissed enough to want revenge. If so, the close call with the *Hercules* could be more than corporate intimidation, it might be a promise of things to come.

But as unsettling as those thoughts were Lando had little time to worry about them because the next couple of days were extremely busy.

They were standard days, and therefore shorter than Snowball's, but still a lot longer than Lando liked. His first task was to move *Junk* down to Orbit Level 4 (OL-4).

Having been properly identified and coded into the ship's recognition system Lando found the controls quite responsive. Though somewhat hampered by his lack of familiarity with the ship's nonstandard systems, Lando found he had little difficulty dropping *Junk* into a lower orbit.

Once *Junk* was established in OL-4 it was a relatively simple matter to match speeds with Utility Platform 63. That's when the real work began.

Junk wasn't a real freighter and didn't have the sort of robotic equipment freighters normally use to load and unload cargo. That meant doing the job by hand, and given the size of *Junk*'s crew, it was a two-day task.

Donning a well-used but still serviceable set of space armor, Lando allowed Melissa to lead him into the lock, and out into the brightly lit launching bay.

"Cap," as Captain Sorenson preferred to be called, and Cy were already there.

Since Cy had his own supply of oxygen, and had his brain tissue safely tucked away inside a metal casing, he had no need of space armor. As a result the cyborg moved freely from atmosphere to vacuum with little or no inconvenience.

Having spent the last hour or so securing various pieces of gear, and preparing the bay to receive cargo, Cy was taking a break. With the ship's argrav turned off to facilitate loading, the little cyborg was busy performing acrobatics and generally making a nuisance of himself.

As Lando stepped out of the lock and into the launching bay, Cy swooped by the pilot's visor and uttered a long drawn-up war whoop over the standard suit-to-suit radio frequency.

Lando swore, Cy laughed, and Melissa broke her contact with the deck in order to give chase.

"There you are," a voice said, and Lando turned to find Captain Sorenson towering above. He was framed by a bright green exoskeleton that stood twelve feet tall and caused Lando's radio to buzz with static.

Sorenson's almost-cheerful manner and flushed face suggested more than a few drinks. Still, the older man was sober enough to do some work, and that was a first.

"Here I am," Lando agreed dryly. "Now what?"

"Now you play catch," the other man answered enigmatically. Cap released himself from the machine and floated free. "Your chariot awaits."

Lando had never had an occasion to use an exoskeleton before, but he understood the theory, and decided it couldn't be that hard. Using the conveniently placed foot supports Lando climbed the exoskeleton's frame until he was even with its shoulders.

Turning, Lando backed into place, aligned his limbs with the machine's, and felt a series of metal bands snap into place around his arms and legs. He flexed his fingers. The exoskeleton did likewise. From now on it would mimic and amplify every motion effectively quadrupling Lando's strength.

"It was designed for maintenance work," Cap said by way of explanation, "but it makes a good catcher."

"Catcher?" Lando asked, moving his right leg experimentally and watching the machine do likewise.

"Yeah," Sorenson answered. "We'll pitch, and you catch.

Pitching takes some practice, so I'm giving the easy job to you."

Lando wanted to ask some more questions but Cap was gone, the jet pak on his back pushing him down through the hatch, with Melissa gamboling along behind.

Moving with great care Lando took a few tentative steps toward the hatch. Electromagnets kept the exoskeleton's podlike feet securely fastened to the deck. Outside of the slight disorientation that came with Lando's increased size, walking was easy.

Looking down through the hatch, Lando saw the lights of Utility Platform 63, and two silhouettes as Cap and Melissa touched down. The space station was huge, half a mile in every direction, and outlined with colored lights.

The platform's function was similar to that of a dirtside warehouse, to store freight prior to shipment, and turn a profit in the process.

Like most of its kind the platform was actually a cube. Freight could be unloaded on any one of the cube's six sides. This was normally accomplished with automated or remote-controlled mini-tugs. A series of concentric circles decorated each landing surface. Once freight was safely deposited in the middle of a bull's-eye, specially designed robots used the zero-G environment to move it down into the platform's interior, where a computerized sorting system put it away. Later, when it was time to load the freight aboard another ship, the process was reversed.

The platform could supposedly handle up to six vessels at once, but that increased the chance of a collision, so Lando was glad that this was a slow rotation. One other ship was present with only the strobe of its navigation lights to separate it from the blackness of space.

"All set?" Cy asked cheerfully, his spherelike body dropping in from Lando's right side. "They oughtta start tossing stuff our way any minute now."

"Here comes!" Cap said, his voice artificially loud over Lando's suit radio. "Time to earn your pay."

Looking down Lando saw a tiny square of reflected light separate itself from the surface of the platform and grow suddenly larger. He watched it like a spectator at first, interested, but outside the action.

"You'd better get ready," Cy cautioned, "it looks like the captain put some zip on that one."

"Some zip?" Lando asked stupidly, and realized the square had grown suddenly larger and was entering the hatch. Now he understood. Using the surface of the platform as an anchor, and zero gravity as a medium, Cap was pitching cargo modules into *Junk*'s hold. Lando's job was to catch them. If he failed they'd ricochet around the inside of the launching bay until they ran out of kinetic energy. That could cause some damage, and, even more important, take his head clean off.

Lando stepped up to the very edge of the hatch and opened his arms.

The cargo module hit the bottom of his right arm, bounced off, and spun to the left. Shuffling in that direction the smuggler made a grabbing motion, managed to capture the plastic case between massive arms, and stood there unsure of what to do next. It was strange to hold a cargo module in his arms. After all, it was six feet long, four feet wide, and four feet deep, and, without the help of the exoskeleton, much too heavy for Lando to lift.

"Heads up!" Cy advised. "Here comes another module. Shove that baby toward me and I'll stow it."

Glancing to his right, Lando saw that Cy had positioned himself in front of the aft section of the bay. Behind him there was an open area. The cargo would be stacked in there.

Lando did as he was instructed, shoving the cargo module toward Cy, and looking down for another. It was already there, a little to the right this time, and tumbling end over end.

As he scrambled to catch it Lando wondered if this was some sort of test, Cap's idea of an initiation, a gut check. If so, Lando decided that he'd show the drunken bastard a thing or two, and threw himself in front of the module. It knocked him backward a step, but he held on, and passed the container to Cy.

After that it became a game, more than that a minor war, with Cap pitching modules as hard as he could and Lando catching them. Finally, after an hour or so, he detected a slight slackening in pace. Grinning to himself, Lando chinned his suit radio and did his best to sound bored.

"What am I supposed to do between modules? Read a book? Let's pick up the pace."

Cap made no answer, but the modules came fast and furious for a while, eventually dropping off to an even slower pace than before.

Six hours later the job was about a third done, and as the crew took a break, Lando was pleased to see that Sorenson looked like death warmed over. It served the old geezer right for playing silly games.

But the break was soon over. A meal, a few hours of sleep, and the whole thing started over. This time it lasted a full day, and by the time it was over, Lando was too tired to enjoy Cap's obvious exhaustion. In fact he sort of admired the older man for having the guts to stick it out. The guy was a drunk, and a poor excuse for a father, but deep down something remained. Something that might even be worth saving.

It reminded Lando of his own father, a smuggler like his father before him, more mystery than person. Lando remembered growing up, time spent with his mother mostly, the two of them waiting for his father's return. Smugglers are gone a lot, picking up and delivering their secret cargoes, so Lando's childhood was filled with a multitude of joyous homecomings and sad departures.

But even the good times were tinged with sadness, because just beneath the surface of his mother's cheerful conversation, there lurked the certainty of tragedy to come. She never talked about it. But with the sixth sense of children everywhere, Lando knew, and his dreams were filled with horror.

Little did Lando know that when tragedy came it would take his mother first. And that when his father died he'd be there to see it. See it and run as fast and far as he could go. But he couldn't outrun the memories and they followed Lando into his dreams.

Lando awoke to the strains of "All Hail the Emperor" piped throughout the ship. It was Cy's idea of humor and Lando's idea of hell. As he stepped into his fresher Lando swore a terrible revenge on the cyborg, but the hot water felt wonderful, and his mood was much improved by the time he emerged.

Thanks to *Junk*'s unorthodox design, Lando's cabin was

much larger than what was found aboard most ships her size, and compared favorably with a Class B suite on a liner. He had a double-sized bunk with overhead storage, a comfortable lounge chair, and a nice desk with built-in comp.

The only thing that bothered him was a vague sense of otherness, as if the space belonged to someone else only recently gone.

Lando raised the question over one of Melissa's instant meals, still in their original containers, and right out of the microwave. The galley was a cheerful space full of white plastic and shiny metal.

Melissa was her usual energetic self, Cap was drawn and haggard, and Cy was elsewhere. Rehydrated mystery strips and simu-eggs don't mean much without digestive organs to process them with.

Lando speared a strip of soggy meat and stuffed it into his mouth. "Gross, Melissa, truly disgusting."

Melissa stuck out her tongue and made a face.

Lando nodded his understanding. "By the way, whatever happened to my predecessor anyway?"

Melissa looked down at the table and fiddled with a burned piece of toast.

Cap scowled and looked up from his coffee. "Dead. A fusion plant aboard one of Sikma's OL-12 habitats blew. We were hired to round up the pieces. You wouldn't believe it, there was junk everywhere, like a cloud of metal it was. Big chunks of it, tumbling end over end, and colliding with anything that got in the way."

Cap gestured with his coffee cup. "Some of it was quite valuable. A few tanks of zero-G biologicals had escaped the explosion and were floating free. We tried to grab them but they were too small. The tanks didn't have enough mass for the tractor beams to lock on to. Lia, she was our pilot, went out to round them up by hand. She zigged when she should have zagged. A free-floating I-beam took her head right off."

Melissa made a sobbing sound and ran from the room. Cap looked back to Lando and shrugged. "Mel hired Lia, so even though it wasn't her fault, she feels responsible. I told her to let it go . . . but she won't. Reminds me of her mother. Just part of growing up I guess."

Hot words boiled up to fill Lando's throat, words about fathers who force little girls to make adult decisions, words about alcoholics who turn their children into parents.

But Lando knew the words could not be heard or understood so he choked them down. Ignoring Cap's curious stare, Lando dropped his fork and left the galley. Sorenson was right about one thing. It wasn't her fault. He'd find Melissa and tell her that.

4

The One Who Falls Upward was tall and skinny as Finthians go, his multicolored plumage somewhat obscured by ceramic body armor and a heavy leather harness. The harness supported a variety of hand weapons. The One Who Falls Upward fingered a worn-looking blaster and watched the screen with large saucerlike eyes. The ship was a three-dimensional cylinder surrounded by three-dimensional spheroids. A few short minutes from now the ship would enter his carefully constructed ambush.

And the Finthian knew lots about the ship, information he would've paid dearly for, but the cyborg offered for free. Well, not for free, since Willer wanted the ship's commanding officer, but almost for free.

"Hold . . . hold . . . almost there . . ." The words came from the translator at the Finthian's neck and found their way into space a fraction of a second later.

Outside, beyond the thick durasteel hull, thirty-one men and women waited to attack. Some clung to smaller asteroids. Others floated free, powered down to escape *Junk*'s scanners, doing their best to imitate pieces of free-floating rock.

All were mounted on hand-built single-seat fighters. No two were alike. Some were souped-up space scooters, others were ex-maintenance sleds, and many were cobbled together from odds and ends.

But all had one thing in common. They were armed to the teeth. Energy weapons, guided missiles, even a smart bomb or two. The incoming ship was as good as dead. The pirates grew impatient.

The One Who Falls Upward understood this, and soothed them as a Dwik Master soothes his hell hounds. "Patience, my children, patience. The wind rewards those who wait."

"The wind blows straight from your ass," a male voice said, but the Finthian ignored him, and the pirates continued to wait.

The One Who Falls Upward glanced to the right and left. The glowing vid screens, the banks of brightly lit controls, and the well-disciplined crew were all part of his design. As was the ancient ore barge that served as his headquarters.

Creaky though it was the barge had its own in-system drive. That, plus a thick layer of real rock, made the barge into a mobile asteroid. A perfect disguise for working the belt, and one that had proved itself many times before.

And now, with the addition of the incoming tug, the Finthian would have a ship equipped with hyperdrive as well. After that, who knows? A destroyer? A cruiser? Anything was possible.

The One Who Falls Upward grinned a predatory grin and returned his attention to the screen. Humans are unpredictable, and one must watch them constantly.

Had he missed anything? No, he'd selected the location with care. The ambush was inside the asteroid belt, but not so far in as to be dangerous.

Over time the gravitational pull of Durna's larger planets caused asteroids to change orbits and collide. The collisions gave birth to more asteroids, or chunks of asteroids, in a never-ending cycle. A violent cycle. That's why it made more sense to steal from the roid miners than to *be* one.

Another reason The One Who Falls Upward had chosen this particular site for his ambush was the system of "gates." There were twenty-seven of them altogether, carefully chosen points where conditions were fairly stable, and the roid miners could enter or leave the belt in relative safety.

Each gate was located in close proximity to an asteroid large enough to survive a minor collision. By placing transmitters on twenty-seven such planetoids the roid miners created an informal navigation system. It wasn't perfect, but it helped a lot when some miner was trying to get home with a holed hull, or a shaky drive.

Unfortunately the system worked in favor of the rock pirates as well, since it allowed them to prepare an ambush at any of the twenty-seven gates, and do so with a good chance of success.

The miners knew this and countered with occasional Q-ships. Q-ships were heavily armed destroyers disguised to look like freighters. The pirates would attack them, take a terrible beating, and run off to lick their wounds.

But time would pass and the pirates would return. Like right now. The ship called *Junk* was easing through the gate. *Junk*! How like the humans! A ship, any ship, deserves a true name. He would name it *The Wind Which Pushes All Before It*, and give it honor.

When he spoke the Finthian's voice was no more than a whisper. "Hold my children . . . hold. The ship is almost there . . ."

Lando squirmed in his seat. The possibility of an ambush was very much on his mind as *Junk* passed through Gate Eighteen and entered the belt.

The trip from Snowball to the asteroid belt had taken three standard days. Simple days during which Lando was free from fear. There were no cargo modules to catch, no bounty hunters to escape, and no police to throw him in jail.

Not until Gate Eighteen that is. Now Lando felt a lead weight riding low in his stomach.

Though not a warship, *Junk* was well armed. Her weapons, and weapons control systems, had been stripped from a pirate cruiser. A *real* pirate cruiser, not one of the flying jokes the rock pirates used.

For reasons unknown the pirates had dropped into the Durna system for a look around, ran smack dab into an Imperial battlewagon, and lost the ensuing battle.

Picking the resulting wreck up for a song, Melissa's mother had salvaged about fifteen percent of the cruiser's weapons, and installed them in *Junk*. Even fifteen percent of a cruiser's total weaponry is a lot for a tug so *Junk* was well armed.

Lando knew this but it did little to reassure him. Weapons are one thing, but competent operators are another, and given *Junk*'s crew they were few and far between.

Okay, assume Cap was sober, a questionable proposition but assume it anyway. He was ensconced in the top weapons turret, and if the pirates attacked, he might give a good account of himself. Fine. That left Melissa and Cy. Melissa was stationed in the port weapons blister, and Cy in the starboard. A little girl and a floating brain. How would they do? Sweat trickled down Lando's back as he watched the scanners.

The One Who Falls Upward hooked taloned thumbs into his harness. It was now or never. "Attack!" As the word left his beak thirty-one fighters launched themselves in *Junk*'s direction.

The fighters showed up as thirty-one points of light on Lando's plot. The computer quickly assigned each one a threat value, a target number, and requested permission to fire.

Lando swore, released the ship's automatic weapons systems, and yelled over the intercom. "Thirty plus incoming hostiles. Engage with secondaries. Engage with secondaries."

As *Junk*'s primary weapons lashed out they killed seven pirates in two seconds. Lando smiled. It was a turkey shoot so far. Another few seconds and the pirates would be history.

The smile faded as a hundred points of light blossomed within the tac tank. What the hell? Then he realized what they were, some kind of decoys, meant to draw fire from the ship's primary armament while allowing the fighters to close untouched.

And it was working. All along *Junk*'s hull energy weapons burped light and auto launchers hurled missiles at bogus targets.

Meanwhile the real pirates were firing and scoring hits that weren't likely to destroy the tug but were doing damage nonetheless.

"Ignore the new targets," Lando shouted over the intercom. "They're fakes! Fire on all targets numbered thirty or lower."

Then Lando ordered the primary weapons systems to do likewise. The ship's fire control computer classified his order as an operator error and continued to fire at the bogus targets.

Deep within his converted ore barge The One Who Falls Upward allowed himself a tiny moment of triumph. The ruse had worked! Eighty-four percent of his custom-made decoys had activated on command. Even now they were destroying themselves, and in the process generating enough heat and electronic activity to resemble a small ship.

Of course skilled use of the ship's secondary armament could still win the battle, but Willer had assured him that the ship was woefully undercrewed, and that would work to his advantage. Without the tug's secondary armament to stop them his fighters would close in and lock themselves to *Junk*'s hull. A few minutes with a torch, a quick death for most of the ship's crew, and *The Wind Which Pushes All Before It* would be his.

The decoys made the tac tank hard to read. Lando's fingers tapped out a quick rhythm and dozens of lights disappeared leaving only those with numbers thirty or lower. There were eighteen left. The pirates could have destroyed *Junk* by now but they wanted the ship intact.

Lando saw one, then another light wink out, as Cap and Cy scored solid hits. Melissa was firing but hadn't hit anything. That meant the port side of the ship was virtually undefended.

Lando had responsibility for the belly. A blip lit up his targeting screen. Almost without thinking he squeezed the control grip and watched the blip disappear.

"I got one!" It was Melissa's voice, but the hit came way too late. By now the pirates had identified the ship's weak side and were swarming to attack it.

Lando was desperate. He considered a random hyperspace jump and rejected it. It might work, but what if it didn't? What if it dumped them in the middle of Durna's sun? No, he needed something with a better chance of success.

Lando checked the nav screens. The huge irregular shapes of asteroids hemmed him in on every side. Damn, if only there was room to run. By now it was obvious the pirates had little more than scooters. *Junk* could outrun them on quarter power.

Wait a minute, what was that? It looked like a huge doughnut with an off-center hole. It was crazy and probably impossible but . . .

A klaxon went off and Cap's voice came over the intercom. "That was me. I burned one just as he touched down on our hull. Run for the speedster, Mel . . . I'll . . ."

Lando didn't wait for more. As his fist slammed down on the emergency power button, his body was pushed back into the seat, his vision began to fade. Fighting to see, Lando watched the doughnut grow bigger and bigger until its edges disappeared off-screen.

The three-dimensional tunnel loomed ahead. Lando fought for control. One little mistake, one touch of the ship's hull to the tunnel's rocky walls, and the ship would tumble out of control. Lando ignored the vids in favor of the nav screen. The computerized graphics were easier to use.

Seconds turned into minutes and minutes into hours. And then, with one final flick of his wrist, they were out and into one of the holes or "lakes" that dotted the belt.

Lando reduced power and checked the tac tank. Nothing. The surviving pirates were back on the other side of the doughnut, unable, or unwilling, to give pursuit.

Lando let out a huge sigh of relief, dumped all systems to standby, and asked the ship for a damage report. A long list had just started to flood Lando's screens when Cap dropped into the co-pilot's seat. The older man looked gray and shaken. There was a forced steadiness to his voice.

"Well done, lad. Next time, however, a little warning would be appreciated."

"Sorry," Lando replied shakily. "There wasn't time."

Cap nodded understandingly. "It was the best piece of piloting I've ever seen. How did you know the hole was big enough?"

"The truth is," Lando answered, "I *didn't* know."

The older man took a moment to absorb this, checked to see if Lando was serious, and laughed. Lando joined him, and by the time Melissa and Cy reached the bridge, both men were laughing hysterically.

Thirty-six hours later *Junk* eased in next to an asteroid named Keeber's Knob. The "knob" was a bulbous rock formation that stuck up from the planetoid's surface, and Keeber was the famous Maxine Keeber, one of the few roid miners to actually strike it rich.

The "Knob," as her fellow miners called the asteroid, contained a high concentration of chalcocite, an excellent source of copper, and therefore quite valuable. Even though copper was one of the most ancient metals used by man it was also one of the most useful.

Rather than mine the chalcocite herself, Maxine had the good sense to sell the asteroid to Perez Mining, the small but growing company that now owned it.

As Lando scanned the vid screens he saw a good-sized roid, maybe two hundred miles in diameter, half in the sun and half out. The company had just enough spin on rock to generate some internal gravity and keep things comfortable. Lando watched the surface rotate from light to dark. As it did the pilot saw enough weapons emplacements to repel anything short of a massed assault by Imperial marines.

As if to reinforce this impression the voice that came over the com link was lazy and self-assured. "Hello, ship. Perez Mining here. You have five seconds to say something we approve of. After that you're free metal."

Cap stepped up to the control panel and touched a switch. "Cut the crap, Tobias. You know who we are. How many ships look like *Junk?*"

"True enough, Cap," the other man replied cheerfully, "but ships change hands sometimes, so it pays to check. I'd ask how you're doing . . . except it's obvious. You're obnoxious as hell."

"I'm obnoxious?" Cap demanded with feigned outrage. "How can a man with the personality of a Zerk Monkey's rear end call *me* obnoxious?"

The banter went on for some time but Lando tuned it out. He had things to do. First he programmed *Junk's* NAVCOMP to keep the ship on the same relative course as the asteroid.

Then Lando went below to prepare the tender for use as a shuttle. Unlike the zero-G-to-zero-G transfer off Snowball, this situation would involve some light gravity as the cargo neared the asteroid's surface, enough to spread the cargo all over the landscape unless they used the tender to ease the landing. Lando was in the process of unhooking a fuel hose from a receptacle in the tender's belly when Melissa appeared.

"Hello, Pik."

"Hello, Melissa. Watch out for the hose."

Melissa jumped out of the way and trudged along behind as Lando pulled it over against a bulkhead. "Are you mad at me?"

Lando dropped the hose and looked down at her. He saw a tremble in her lower lip and eyes that were shiny with barely controlled tears. "Of course not. Why would I be mad at you?"

"Because I screwed up. I tried, I really did, but I couldn't hit them. Except for one, and that was luck."

Lando sat down on a crate of spare parts. He winked. "A hit's a hit. When you win, always take credit for it, and when you lose, blame it on bad luck."

Melissa gave a wan smile. "You're trying to make me feel better. Mom said I should take responsibility for my actions." Melissa looked down at her feet. "And I screwed up. If it weren't for you . . . we'd be dead."

Lando wanted to hug her but held himself back. Hugs were her father's job whether he did it or not. He cleared his throat.

"Tell me something, Melissa. Let's say Cy wasn't here . . . and the ship's drives were out of alignment. I try to fix them and fail. Is that my fault?"

Melissa looked thoughtful. "No, since you aren't an engineer, it's not your fault. You did the best you could."

Lando nodded. "Right. So ask yourself the following questions. Are you an adult? Are you a trained gunner? And did you do the best you could?"

Melissa thought about it for a moment, wiped her face with a sleeve, and smiled. "Thanks, Pik. Daddy says you're one helluva pilot . . . but you're something more too. You're my best friend." And with that Melissa kissed Lando's cheek, laughed, and skipped away.

It took three standard days to transfer the cargo from *Junk* to the planetoid below. Over and over they loaded cargo aboard the tender, ferried it down to Knob's surface, and dragged it onto the crawlers that carried it away. The miners provided some of the muscle but it was still hard work, and by the time it was over, Lando was ready for two or three days of rest. Unfortunately he didn't get them.

Once the final load of cargo was down the miners threw a party in their underground complex. It was a cheerful affair, complete with games for the children and an open bar for the adults.

Melissa had a wonderful time, whooping and screaming as the children chased each other up and down the duracrete corridors, and whining when it was time to leave.

Cy won twenty credits in a game of Rockets and Stars, Cap drank until he passed out, and Lando hit on a pretty brunette named Cee.

She had quick intelligent eyes, a stiff mohawk, and a very nice figure. As usual Lando tried some of his father's favorite smuggling stories first, got a good reaction, and went for the close. "How 'bout you and I slip away and talk?"

It didn't work. Cee patted his hand as she spoke. "Thanks, Pik, but there's three things I never do: I never play with loaded guns, I never go outside without a suit, and I never go to bed with pilots. Call me conservative . . . but that's how I am."

So as they pulled away from Knob, Lando was more than a little hung over, still horny, and looking forward to some rest. All he had to do was find a gate, pass through it, and punch in Snowball's coordinates. Then, barring rock pirates and other unforeseen problems, they could coast all the way home.

Lando was just setting up a course for Gate Twelve when Cap staggered onto the bridge. His hair was uncombed, his eyes were red, and he moved as if his body were made of glass. Coming up behind Lando he examined the vid screens, checked *Junk*'s course, and offered the pilot a data cube.

"Looks fine . . . but run this course instead. Call me if you see anything unusual." So saying, the older man turned and walked away.

Somewhat surprised, Lando accepted the cube, and began to plug it in. He stopped when he heard Cap's voice. "Lando?"

The pilot turned around. Cap was more than halfway to the starboard lift tube. "Yeah?"

"You'll call me if you see anything strange?"

"Yeah, Cap. I'll call you."

"Good." And with that Cap walked away.

Curious, Lando plugged the cube into the NAVCOMP, pulled it on-line, and read it out. He frowned as the screen filled with orderly rows of numbers. The numbers disappeared as his fingers danced over a keyboard. A pattern appeared. A graphic layout of the belt's known features, the gates, and Cap's course.

It didn't make any sense. Sorenson's course would cause them to crisscross a small section of the belt a dozen times. In doing so they would risk collision with uncharted debris, use a lot of fuel, and waste what could've been productive time. It was a stupid thing to do. No wonder Cap was broke, or the next closest thing.

"Weird, huh?"

Lando went for his slug gun as he turned around.

Cy squirted himself backward and dipped apologetically. "Sorry, Pik. I'll make some noise next time."

Lando nodded, somewhat mollified, but unwilling to let Cy completely off the hook. "I should think so. That's a damn good way to get yourself blasted."

The cyborg rotated forward in agreement. "Sorry, Pik. It won't happen again."

Lando smiled. Something about Cy made it hard to stay mad. Besides, the cyborg was a good sort, and one helluva engineer. By working damned near around the clock Cy had repaired most of the damage done during the pirate attack. "You said Cap's course was 'weird' . . . as if you were expecting it."

The silver ball made a jerking motion that reminded Lando of a shrug. "I was. Every time we enter the belt, Cap waits till the job's done, and searches for his ship."

"Ship? What ship?"

Cy floated toward the control panel and came to rest on top of the tac tank. "You remember that cyborg named Jord Willer? The one that damned near rammed us off Snowball? Remember how he mentioned the *Star of Empire*? Well, she was a liner, a big one. The biggest of her time. I even rode on her once when I was a little boy, but that was more than thirty standards back, and before Cap took command. She was a grand ship, nearly four miles long, and loaded with every luxury you can imagine.

"Every year the *Empire* made a tour of the inner planets. And every year two thousand members of the social elite would pay exorbitant prices to come aboard, criticize each other's clothes, and enjoy 'the tour.' "

Cy was silent for a moment, as if collecting his thoughts, or remembering how it felt to have a flesh-and-blood body.

"Anyhow, the way Cap tells it, the *Star of Empire* was in hyperspace, making the jump from New Britain to a nav beacon just off Durna's sun when something went wrong.

"Nobody knows for sure, but Cap thinks that a billion-to-one failure by the NAVCOMP dropped the ship out of hyperspace a fraction of a second too early. Others believe it was a tiny drive fluctuation, or some sort of unusual discontinuity in hyperspace, but whatever the reason . . . she came out right in the middle of the asteroid belt."

Now Lando remembered. He remembered adults talking, some sort of distant disaster, and the name: *Star of Empire*.

He looked at Cy. "If Cap was in command, what's he doing here?"

Cy swiveled from side to side as if shaking his head. "Come on, Pik! When you lose a ship like the *Empire,* your career is over, no matter where you are at the time. And if you're dead drunk, well, a tug's the most you can hope for."

"Cap was drunk?"

Cy rolled forward, then back. "That's right. The first officer got some of the people off, including Cap, but very few survived. Many of those who survived the initial impact with the roid were killed while trying to escape the belt."

Lando tried to imagine. A huge ship, miles long, suddenly appears in the middle of an asteroid belt and crashes into a roid. There's chaos as passengers are sucked into space and klaxons hoot too late.

Men scream as they fight for lifeboats.

Children die as metal bends inward to crush soft flesh.

Corridors are slick with blood.

Air whistles out through a tiny hole as a man struggles to plug it.

An old man smiles and plays the grand piano in the ship's lounge.

An officer yells orders until a passenger kills her, takes her space armor, and heads for a lock.

Lovers embrace as the air is sucked from their lungs.

And somewhere in all this a drunk captain, a limp load over someone's shoulder, wakes to find that his ship is dead.

Lando shook his head in amazement. "So what're you telling me? That Cap's looking for the *Star*?"

"That's right," Cy replied. "There was a lot of confusion after the wreck. Lifeboats went every which way. Many were never seen again. With the exception of Cap and Jord Willer, the entire bridge crew was killed. The ensuing investigation took two years, the trial took months, but they never found the wreck.

"That was thirty years ago, and most people figure she's been pounded into a billion pieces by now, but not Cap. No, he thinks she's a drifter, a ghost ship waiting for his return.

"It takes him a while to get drunk, and if you catch him at just the right point, he'll tell you all about it. For that matter he'll tell the *entire* bar about it. How she's out there, a drifter worth millions in salvage, just waiting for someone to claim her."

Lando remembered Jord Willer, and his promise to be there when Cap found the *Star*. The cyborg wanted more than revenge, he wanted millions in salvage as well.

Cy chuckled. "Yeah, Cap wants her all right, but it's more than money he wants. It's his honor. He left it aboard that ship . . . and he wants it back."

"What's Daddy want?" Melissa said, putting a coffee flask next to Lando's elbow.

"The *Star of Empire*," Cy replied.

"Oh, that," Melissa said, instantly bored. "That's a waste of time . . . but Mommy said to humor him."

Lando poured a cup of coffee and held it up in a salute. "And we shall. First I'll have a cup of this excellent coffee . . . and then we're off. Ghost hunters extraordinaire."

Melissa laughed and the conversation turned mundane.

But outside, beyond the strength of *Junk*'s hull, the asteroids continued to whirl and dance. A dance as vast as the solar system itself, as precise as the laws that governed it, and as relentless as time. A dance of secrets kept.

5

Lando wrinkled his nose. The air smelled of ozone, peat smoke, and animal droppings. Not a pleasant mix, but a real one, and preferable to the recycled stuff aboard ship.

Stepping onto a new planet never failed to excite him. New sights, new sounds, and, yes, new smells no matter how pungent. All were a part of the newness. All were welcome. A light breeze touched Lando's cheek and he smiled.

Dista was close to Earth normal, with only a slightly longer day and a touch more gravity. As a result humans felt quite comfortable and, lured by Imperial land grants, were still arriving. That accounted for the fact that the planet boasted three new spaceports.

This one, a largely prefab affair located just outside Dista's largest city, looked just like many others all over the empire. A large repulsor-blackened expanse of duracrete, a scattering of grounded ships, and a utilitarian control-maintenance facility. If you've seen one, you've seen 'em all.

But when visitors stepped out through the spaceport's gates, they took a step backward in time. The effect was so startling that many paused to look around. Lando was no exception. The view was amazing.

At the same time that high-flying shuttles left streaks across the upper atmosphere, Dib-drawn carts creaked down rutted roads, and peat fires pointed smoky fingers toward the sky.

"Hey, Pik! Come on! We haven't got all day!"

The voice belonged to Cap. He and Melissa were a hundred feet up ahead, skillfully sidestepping the dome-shaped piles of Dib dung, and motioning for Lando to hurry.

Cy was still aboard ship, but both of the Sorensons were

dirtside, and eager to reach town. Cap had some business to transact and Melissa wanted to play. Lando waved in response and hurried to catch up.

It was market day, and that meant a constant stream of foot traffic, Dib-drawn carts, and crawlers moving into town. They carried everything from produce to freshly cut peat. As the vehicles moved they stirred the mud with Dib droppings and sprayed the resulting mixture over everything in sight.

At first Lando tried to stay clean, but it was a hopeless task, and he soon gave up. By the time Lando caught up with the others he was as muddy and messy as they were.

A cart squeaked by and sprayed guck on his pants leg. Melissa laughed, Cap looked impatient, and the three of them headed for town.

Looking around, Lando saw that the settlers wore similar clothes. Their favorite combination consisted of synthetic trousers, some sort of long-sleeved shirt, and a leather jerkin.

Lando noticed that most of the settlers wore side arms. Not the silly ones that look like jewelry, but real weapons, shiny with use and carefully maintained. Did they use them on each other or the local wildlife? Either way they made a tough-looking crowd and Lando decided to watch his step.

At first Lando had refused to come, pleading poverty and pretending little interest. The truth was that he was secretly afraid of the bounty hunters who might be waiting for him on Dista's surface.

But five boring days spent searching the asteroid belt for a ghost ship had left Lando yearning for some bright lights. Or even some dim ones. That, plus Melissa, had finally changed his mind.

The campaign started soon after Cap announced Dista as their next port of call. Almost immediately Melissa began to tell Lando stories about how pretty Dista was, how friendly the settlers were, and what a good time he'd have dirtside.

Melissa put lots of energy into her arguments, looked very sincere, and didn't fool Lando for a moment. It wasn't him she wanted, it was any adult.

Melissa was afraid that once on the surface her father would get falling down drunk, pass out, and need help. More help than she could give. And seeing her fear Lando agreed to come.

A row of shacks had sprung into existence to either side of the road, and up ahead more substantial buildings could be seen, their solid log walls ready to repel anything short of a force ten hurricane.

Lando smiled when he saw the sign that identified the muddy path as Port Town's "Main Street," but the smile faded when he saw the boardwalks and the people who lined them.

They were predators looking for prey. As different from the townspeople who moved around them as night is from day. There were con artists looking for marks, pimps looking for Johns, gamblers looking for suckers, and, yes, bounty hunters looking for him. Well, not *him* specifically, but anyone with a price on his head.

They sat on rickety chairs, lounged against walls, and engaged each other in desultory conversation. But Lando noticed their eyes were everywhere, checking, comparing, and evaluating potential prey.

Lando turned away and started a one-sided conversation with Cap. Cap's mind was elsewhere, so he answered with a series of semi-articulate grunts and seemed annoyed.

Melissa was everywhere, running circles around them and asking all sorts of questions.

Meanwhile Lando could *sense* memprinted images of his face flashing into the surrounding minds, could *feel* blasters lining up on his back, could *hear* a voice shouting, "Hey you! Pik Lando! Stop or die!"

But the shout never came, and a few minutes later they had entered another part of town, a section where the feel was entirely different. Here huge warehouses lined both sides of the street, the mud was even deeper, and heavy equipment growled about.

"Here it is," Cap said, coming to a sudden stop next to some wooden stairs.

A somewhat faded sign announced, "Lois Joleen, Shipping Agent."

Cap shifted his weight from one foot to the other. "Here's hoping she's got some work for us. You two have a good time."

"We'll see you at the port?" Melissa said hopefully.

Lando saw the look in her eyes and knew what she was thinking. If her father met them at the spaceport, there was less chance that he'd show up drunk.

"Naw," Cap answered carelessly. "Town would be more convenient. That way we can walk back together. Let's meet across from the Port City Mercantile at 1600 hours. Don't be late."

Melissa smiled, apparently reassured. "We won't. Come on, Pik! I'll race you to the vidplex!"

The two men exchanged a smile, and Cap watched for a moment as Lando followed Melissa toward the center of town. The pilot seemed like a nice sort, Mel certainly took to him, and that was good.

Cap felt a stab of guilt. He should spend more time with her. Give her some sort of normal life where she could play with other children. Sell *Junk* and settle down. But that would mean becoming a ground pounder, giving up the one thing he did right, and abandoning all hope of finding the *Star of Empire*.

The thoughts weighed heavily as Cap climbed the muddy stairs and paused to clean his boots.

A section of metal grating had been installed in the middle of the top landing, along with a raised metal bar and a short section of hose. By alternately scraping his boots on the bar, and squirting them with the hose, Cap removed the worst of the mud.

A wooden mallet hung by a length of chain from the wall. Cap used it to hit the heavy wooden door three times.

He had no idea why Lois Joleen chose this particular kind of door knocker. It was just one of her many eccentricities, and compared to the rest, hardly worth mention.

There was a loud click as the door lock was released. Cap gave the door a gentle push and it swung open. There was no one there to greet him nor had he expected anyone. Joleen worked alone, or Cap assumed that she did, because in all the times that he'd come to visit he'd never seen anyone else.

Her office was full of junk, all kinds, without apparent rhyme or reason. A sort of trail led back toward Joleen's office. As Cap followed it he saw oxygen tanks, robo parts, a portable generator, coils of high-tension cable, boxes of dried fruit, hand tools, and much, much more. Did she sell it? Collect it? Cap had no idea.

Joleen's office was a semi-open area in the sea of junk. Light was provided by an expensive lamp with a built-in antigrav unit. By way of contrast her desk was made from planks of wood laid across a couple of sawhorses and held together with a few sloppily driven nails.

There was nothing sloppy about the computer that sat on it, however. It was a Nigunda 4001, with built-in com center and enough processing power to run the whole planet. Which, Cap reflected, she probably did, though indirectly.

Joleen looked up at Cap's approach. She had a long, narrow face. Her bushy black eyebrows, large nose, and hard, straight mouth gave her a hard, aggressive look.

"So, looking for some work, eh?"

Cap gave her a twisted smile. "Maybe. Or maybe I came to see you."

Joleen gave a snort of derision. "That'll be the day! Plop your butt down and have a drink. You still drink, don't you?" Her eyes had a hard, challenging look that Cap managed to avoid.

"Don't mind if I do." Cap sat down on a hard stool, accepted a half-empty bottle of Dista Mist, and poured the amber fluid into a dirty glass. The whiskey went down smooth as silk and made a warm pool in Cap's stomach. He poured another glass. "So how's business?"

Joleen shrugged and rested her chin on large, rough hands. "I can't complain. How'd the run into the belt go?"

Cap downed the second drink and noticed that the bottle had disappeared. "Fine. We ran into some trouble going in. Rock pirates. We got through though."

Joleen nodded. "I heard. It sounds like you've got a hot pilot."

Cap looked at her suspiciously but it did him little good. Joleen's face was a mask. How did she know about Lando? Did she have spies among the pirates? Among the miners on Keeber's Knob? With Joleen anything was possible.

"Yeah, he's good all right, better than we deserve. So what's up? You have anything for us?"

Joleen stood up. She was about six-two, long and skinny, dressed frontier style in pants and jerkin. Two steps carried her to a side table. It was piled high with printouts, fire extinguishers, and reels of brightly colored wire. Joleen rummaged around for a moment, located what she was looking for, and returned.

Cap accepted the printout, opened it up, and found himself looking at an orbital schematic for Pylax. Thanks to its rich mineral deposits Pylax had been settled before Dista and was more industrialized.

Cap searched the schematic for some sort of meaning and came up empty. "So?"

"So look again," Joleen said patiently. "Look at the plot points for orbital junk. You'll see quite a few."

Cap did as he was told and found she was right. Most planets had at least some junk in orbit, worn-out satellites, abandoned habitats, fuel tanks, cargo modules, wrecks, you name it. But scanning the schematic Cap saw that Pylax had more than its fair share.

Each piece of debris was marked with a dot, an orbit designator such as OL-23, and a serial number that set it off from functional satellites, habitats, and ships. The serial numbers were consecutive but scattered all around the globe. The highest one that Cap saw was D-1,247. That meant there were at least 1,247 pieces of junk in orbit around Pylax and maybe more. More than enough to be a hazard to navigation and justify the cost of a cleanup.

Cap saw where Joleen was headed. He looked her in the eye. "Come on, Lois . . . there's got to be something better than this. A tow, a salvage job, something."

Joleen shook her head. "I'm sorry, Cap, I really am, but you know how it is. The big companies like Stellar Tug & Salvage get the really lucrative jobs. They have lots of clout and pay heavy-duty kickbacks. It stinks, but that's how the system works. Still, I wouldn't turn my nose up at the Pylax job, it pays pretty well."

"How well is 'pretty well'?"

"Fifty thousand credits, minus my ten percent, makes it worth forty-five. That, plus salvage rights to anything worth the trouble."

Cap brightened a little. Most of the stuff would be close to worthless, but somewhere among those 1,247 pieces of junk there had to be a valuable nugget or two, and that could make all the difference. Some quick mental arithmetic informed him that the forty-five was just enough to pay off current debts, fuel the ship, and operate for the next two months. It wasn't great, but that's all there was.

"Okay, I'll take it."

"Good," Joleen said evenly. "Half up front and half on completion."

"No way," Cap countered. "I've got expenses. Seventy-five percent up front, and twenty-five on completion."

"You're out of your mind," Joleen responded pleasantly. "Two-thirds up front, with a third on completion."

"Deal," Cap said, and stuck out his hand.

Joleen pumped it once and offered a rare smile. "You drive a hard bargain, Cap, but not as hard as Mel. She'd have held out for the full seventy-five."

Della Dee stepped into the saloon and looked around. It was one big open room, with a wooden bar that ran the length of one wall and a huge fireplace. The air smelled of peat, tobacco, and the sweet reek of dope sticks. Two dozen pairs of eyes swiveled around to look her over. Those that were male liked what they saw and took another look.

Dee was about five-ten, shapely, and dressed in a blue one-piece ship-suit. She also wore the top half of some flat-black ceramic body armor, a slug gun in a cross-draw holster, and knee-high boots.

But none of these things accounted for the interested looks. Those resulted from her flaming red hair. It surrounded her face like a frame, shining waves of red, which fell gently to her shoulders. That plus bright green eyes set in flawless white skin caught and held their gaze.

Careful to avoid eye contact Dee scanned the faces and found nothing but the usual mix of barroom scum. Not too surprising all things considered.

Dee moved and most of the eyes broke away. But a few followed, and as Dee headed toward an empty corner, she felt them running up and down her body.

There was a small table and two chairs. Dee chose the one that would put her back to the corner. Then she waited for the first one to arrive. It didn't take long.

He was tall and fairly good-looking, the kind that did well with women, and expected easy pickings. He had a glass of Dista Mist in each hand and put them down without asking her permission.

"Name's Brodie . . . thought I'd buy you a drink."

Dee sighed. It was always the same. The red hair was like a magnet. Or better yet a flame, a flame that attracted every insect around. "The name's Dee . . . and I don't want it."

Brodie sat down. "Sure you do. It's prime stuff. Try it."

Dee smiled. "Do you feel something touching your crotch?"

The man frowned. "Yeah . . . but it doesn't feel like your hand."

Dee nodded her agreement. "That's right, bozo. Now listen carefully. I don't want your drink. I don't want you. Go tell your friends a lie. Tell 'em I'm meeting you later, tell 'em I'm a guy in drag, tell 'em anything you want. But do it now . . . or I'll blow your balls off."

Brodie gulped, turned suddenly white, and stood up. For a moment he considered some bluster, a statement to salve his wounded ego, but something about the expression on Dee's face froze the words in his throat. As he turned and walked away Brodie was organizing a story for his friends.

The two glasses of Dista Mist were still where Brodie had left them. Not wishing to see such a valuable substance go to waste, Dee tossed one off and nursed the other.

She gave the room one more scan, hoping to see a face that matched her memory, knowing it was unlikely. Still, a bounty hunter's work is never done, and you never know when a piece of crud will float to the surface right in front of you. The place was full of creeps but none with a price on their heads. Dee would wait.

Waiting was something she knew how to do. As a little girl she'd waited for someone to show up at the state-run orphanage and take her home. As a marine she'd waited for a purpose that never came. As a woman she'd waited for a man who never showed up. So what the hell, she had all day, and could wait a little longer.

Lando had expected something primitive, something in keeping with Dista's undeveloped landscape, but the vidplex was quite sophisticated. It seemed that the settlers, and especially their children, were hungry for the pleasures left behind.

Sensing an opportunity to cash in on that hunger, a local entrepreneur had put together a full-scale entertainment center, complete with neurogames, holodramas, and compuplays.

The compuplays were Melissa's favorite. They took place

in a large open space. For a fee, each participant received an audio compulink, a costume, and a starting position somewhere in the room.

Then, when sufficient players had been signed up, the computer would take them through a play. Sometimes it was a classic, sometimes contemporary, and sometimes entirely ad lib.

As the young actors and actresses were prompted through their parts by the computer, holo-projected scenery appeared and disappeared, and a partisan audience clapped their approval.

The bolder and more experienced players often made up lines of their own, and hearing this, the computer would juggle the others to match. The result was a play in which the actors could lean on the computer or use their own imaginations.

A rather involved romantic comedy had just come to a hilarious end, and Melissa, who'd played the part of the female lead's best friend, had just rushed into the viewing stands. Lando smiled at her frenzied approach. She still wore her costume and was beaming from ear to ear. The long-flowing party dress made a swishing noise as she moved.

"Wasn't it funny? Didn't Lisa do a nice job as Margaret? Oh, Pik, I had so much fun! I wish Daddy were here." She put a hand to her ear. "The computer says there's a mystery coming up next . . . can I please?"

Lando looked at his wrist term and shook his head. "I'm sorry, Melissa. We promised to meet your father at 1600 hours and it's 1545 right now. Lose the costume and let's go."

She tried an exaggerated pout. "Please?"

"Nope."

Melissa laughed. "Okay, I'll change and be right back."

Fifteen minutes later they were ankle deep in mud out front of Port City Mercantile. There were people and shaggy-looking Dibs all over the place but no Cap. Lando looked at his wrist term. "We're only five minutes late. He'd wait for us wouldn't he?"

Melissa frowned and looked across the street. Lando followed her gaze. The sign said, "Hizo's Saloon, The Home of Dista Mist." "Chances are he's waiting in there."

Lando wanted to say something, to comfort Melissa, but she avoided his eyes. They were halfway across the street when the cheap glass in the saloon's front window shattered and a body came flying out.

Dee had seen it all a thousand times before. People get drunk, the strong pick on the weak, and fueled by liquid courage, the weak fight back. Such was the case right now.

The whole thing had started with the arrival of a huge chrome-plated cyborg. A weird-looking thing with a human head and a sculpted body. It and a couple of ugly-looking sidekicks had taken up residence at a large table and proceeded to be as obnoxious as possible.

This took the form of drinking, laughing, and poking fun at other customers. Though normally not a healthy thing to do, the cyborg was more than a little intimidating, and no one had chosen to take offense.

And then a strange thing occurred. A tall, skinny man with the look of a ship's officer had entered the saloon, peered around, and taken a seat at the bar.

Dee had given him an automatic scan, dismissed him as a law-abiding citizen, and turned her attention elsewhere. That's when the ruckus began. She missed the start of it, but heard someone shout "Watch out!" and looked over just in time to see the tall, skinny man break a bar stool over the cyborg's head.

While this action would have killed a lesser creature, it didn't even mess the cyborg's blond hair, and he gave a roar of outrage. He charged, the man sidestepped, and all hell broke loose.

Dee wasn't sure how or why, but within seconds the fight had spread to the rest of the bar, and she found herself on the edge of a melee. Having no desire to get beat up, especially for free, Dee stayed in her corner. That's when the face entered the saloon.

Dee thought of him as "the face," because she couldn't remember his name, but remembered his face and knew he was wanted. The only problem was that he was on the far side of a really vicious barroom fight. Not only that, but he had a little girl with him, and that could complicate matters. Dee had done lots of things during her life . . . but greasing children wasn't one of them.

Dee was on her feet and searching for a safe way across

the room when the face yelled something and charged into the crowd. The little girl followed and the two of them were soon lost from sight.

A full five minutes of confusion followed during which Dee fought her way across the room, hitting and kicking, careful to avoid the larger, more powerful combatants. And she was more than halfway there when a momentary lull in the fighting gave her a glimpse of her quarry.

He was on the floor with the cyborg standing over him. The silver monster held a chair over his head, and was just about to bring it down when the face shot him in both knees. Not in the head for a certain kill, but in the knees, so the cyborg toppled like a giant tree.

Unable to walk, the cyborg was still screaming his rage when the face scooped an unconscious figure off the floor, checked to make sure the little girl was okay, and walked out of the saloon.

It was an amazing sight but it cost Dee plenty. The blow was actually meant for someone else, but it hit the side of her head with incredible force and dropped her like a rock. The resulting darkness felt surprisingly good.

6

Lando held his breath as he climbed into the space suit. He'd been living in it for the past two weeks. It was, to use Melissa's phrase, "ripe beyond belief."

Lando had tried everything from soap and water to industrial-strength deodorants and nothing worked. The suit had been around a long time, and over the years the smell of sweat, urine, and God knows what else had worked its way down into hundreds of little nooks and crannies.

Lando's air gave out and he was forced to breathe. The sour coppery smell nearly gagged him. His suit radio crackled into life. "Hey, Pik, how ya doing?"

"Great," Lando lied, "just great. Couldn't be better. Shouldn't you be working on your math?"

"I am," Melissa replied defensively, "I was checking, that's all. That's my job, isn't it?"

"Yeah," Lando replied, snapping the suit's final closure. "That's your job when I'm *outside* the tender. When I'm *inside* the tender your job is math. How're you going to be a pilot if you don't know any math?"

"I'll hire you to do it for me," Melissa responded cheerfully. "Besides, you're just grumpy 'cause you're going outside."

"Sounds like a good enough reason to me," Lando replied.

He hit the large square of green plastic with his gloved fist and waited while the inner hatch irised closed. His external mike picked up the loud whining sound. He'd heard that sound a lot lately, and wished it would go away.

They'd been working on the orbital cleanup job for two weeks now, long tedious weeks, during which he'd spent endless hours on the beam controls.

There were two kinds of beams, tractor beams that could pull things toward the tender, and pressor beams that could push them away.

The trick was to use these beams in conjunction with the ship's sensors to push and pull things into the trap. The work was very exacting. Some pieces of debris were so small the beams had a hard time getting a purchase. Somewhat akin to chasing a pea with two tree trunks.

And then, just to make the task even more interesting, there was the trap itself. It was a large rectangular structure cobbled together by Cap and Cy. Basically it was a durasteel frame covered with metal mesh and equipped with some bolt on steering jets.

A set of remote controls aboard the tender allowed Lando to steer the trap, open and close its various doors, and place objects inside for storage.

Doing so was a challenge since any attempt to capture debris required Lando to control the trap as well as a couple of tractor beams.

Simple for anyone with three hands, but a rather difficult task for everyone else.

And then there was the inspection phase, "panning for gold" Cap called it, which forced Lando to spend a lot of time in his space armor. "Panning for gold" was not only physically demanding it was also dangerous as hell.

The fact was that Lando rarely knew exactly what he was stuffing into the trap. Although the ship's sensors could tell him lots about an item's heat, speed, mass, and density, they couldn't tell him what the object *was*. And since what an object *was* had a lot to do with its potential *value,* someone had to inspect it. More often than not that someone was Lando.

A red light came on to indicate vacuum inside the lock. Lando hit a square of green plastic and waited for the outer door to cycle open. As he did so, Lando hit another switch and killed the electromagnetic wall lock. With no argrav in the tender his suit floated free.

Lando's stomach felt heavy. The odds grew worse each time he went outside. Lots of things could go wrong. His suit could malfunction, he could collide with a piece of orbiting junk, a loose space mine could explode and blow him to smithereens, a chunk of radioactive drive shielding could fry his brains . . . the list went on and on.

All things considered, it was hard to say which he liked less, running from bounty hunters or working for Cap. He could quit of course, but then there was the contract, and the fact that he hadn't been paid.

Lando had approached Cap about his pay on two different occasions, and each time the other man put him off, citing "administrative difficulties," and promising to deal with it soon.

The latest excuse was a need "to do a little banking," and accounted for the fact that Cap had gone dirtside about two hours before.

Lando wondered if the bank was located in close proximity to a bar, and hoped that if Cap got drunk, he wouldn't run into Jord Willer.

Was it simply bad luck that had guided Cap into Hizo's Saloon on Dista? Or had Willer planned it? Waited for Cap to show up and then started the fight?

One thing was for sure. Having shot the cyborg in both of his chrome-plated kneecaps, Lando was safer in space than he would be on the ground, unless he died "panning for gold" of course. The thought was far from cheerful, and Lando did his best to suppress it.

The external door was open and Lando used conveniently located handholds to pull himself toward it. Just inside the hatch he scanned his readouts, checked his monofilament lifeline, and chinned the radio.

"I'm stepping outside for a while. Keep a close eye on the vid screens."

"That's a roger," Melissa answered. "If someone comes our way I'll let you know."

Lando hoped so. Cy had marked off their current search area with radio beacons, but you never knew when some idiot would decide to ignore them. And if they did that, chances were they'd ignore his suit beacon too, and take a shortcut right through the center of his chest.

What were the odds of a ship passing through his chunk of space anyway? Thousands to one? Millions to one? Even "billions to one" sounded dangerous to Lando. He fired his suit jets and headed into space.

Pylax was a dark presence below, a black disk over which the sun was barely starting to rise, rays of brilliant light hitting his visor and causing it to polarize.

Lando cut power and checked his safety line. It was a pain, but given Melissa's limited abilities, his only chance in case of an accident. The other end of the cable was hooked to a power winch inside the lock. If necessary Melissa could reel him in like a fish on a line and then holler for help.

The cable looked fine. Beyond it the tender's multicolored navigation lights blinked on and off with boring regularity.

Lando turned away, fired his suit jets, and headed for the trap. Its corners were marked with flashing red beacons. Sunlight gleamed off metal mesh and hinted at shapes within.

It took twelve minutes to make the journey. Once there Lando hooked his lifeline to the wire mesh, went inside, and closed the gate behind him.

Junk rounded up during the previous days had already been stashed in the expandable compartment located at what Lando thought of as the trap's stern. Being little more than a box made of durasteel and wire mesh, the trap didn't actually have a bow or stern, but what the heck, he could call it the stern if he wanted to.

Lando took a deep breath and began the tedious process of sorting, inspecting, and securing his latest finds. He dealt with large items first. Unlike the smaller stuff they were easy to get his hands on, easy to check out, and easy to move.

There was all the usual stuff. Chunks of scrap metal, empty oxy tanks, a broken stabilizer, some cargo pallets, and a worn-out comsat.

Lando had the comsat in front of him, and was pushing it toward the stern, when he saw something from the corner of his eye. He turned and it was gone.

What the hell? Had he imagined it? No, it was a space suit all right, and inside the trap.

The comsat drifted away completely forgotten. Lando pulled his hand blaster and headed toward a piece of free-floating solar panel. Questions jostled each other looking for answers. Who was this guy? Where'd he come from? And what the hell was he doing in the trap?

Sunlight flared off the panel's reflective surface as Lando skimmed across it. His visor grew darker while his suit labored to dump the extra heat. There he was! Sliding behind a shattered cargo module.

"All right you sonovabitch . . . come out with your hands on your helmet!"

"Pik? What's the matter? Who're you talking to?"

Lando gave himself a mental kick in the pants. He'd given himself away and scared Melissa to boot.

"Don't worry, honey, just cover me with that blast rifle, and we'll put him in a cross fire."

As he shot toward the cargo module, Lando gritted his teeth and waited for Melissa to ask, "What blast rifle?"

Much to his surprise the question never came.

Grabbing the cargo module's top edge, Lando pulled himself up and over. The maneuver must have caught his opponent completely off guard, because as Lando grabbed him, the other man didn't resist. "Gotcha!"

"I've got him covered, Pik . . . shall I blast him?" There was a quaver in Melissa's voice that belied her words.

"No need," Lando replied, pressing his blaster against the other man's helmet. "I've got things under control. Okay, bozo . . . talk or suck vacuum. Who the hell are you, and what're you doing here?"

Silence.

Lando started to say something, then changed his mind. There was something weird about this guy, about the way he just hung there, limp as an old dishrag.

Acting on a hunch, Lando turned his helmet light on and aimed it through the other man's visor. What he saw made him gag and push the suit away.

It was horrible. Some stringy hair, a couple of bulging eyes, and a lot of rotting flesh. Not only was this guy dead, he'd been that way for quite a while. Lando's breakfast came up for a visit and he forced it back down.

Then Lando saw something else. Something down low where the man's abdomen would be, a blackened area, where an energy beam had burned its way through the expensive self-sealing suit. A high-powered blaster perhaps . . . or a light energy cannon.

"Pik?"

"It's okay, Melissa. I've been playing hide 'n' seek with a stiff. More in a bit."

Lando heard Melissa's mike click twice in acknowledgment.

A stiff. Damn. There was no way around it. He'd have to collar the corpse and turn it in. Lando could imagine the paperwork, the interviews, the endless bureaucratic nonsense.

Easing his way forward, Lando grabbed a space-suited arm, and pulled the body toward him. He was just about to take the corpse under tow when something flashed in the sun.

Turning the space suit slightly, he saw that there was a comet etched into the top of each shoulder, a golden comet, the kind worn by Imperial Couriers. A courier by God!

With a growing sense of excitement Lando saw that a small satchel was clipped to the courier's chest.

Squeamishness suddenly forgotten, Lando towed the body to the main gate and tied it to the wire mesh. After that it was a simple matter to remove the satchel.

It had no weight due to zero gravity, but the satchel's contents were solid, and tightly packed.

Moving the satchel into the light, Lando saw a series of snap closures, and a wax seal that bore the Imperial crest. Lando knew that he shouldn't open the satchel . . . and knew that he would.

"Watch out," his father had cautioned him years ago. "Curiosity killed a lot of Landos."

Lando used clumsy gloved fingers to break the seal. After that the closures unsnapped one at a time, until the flap was loose, and he could push it out of the way.

Suddenly released, a pair of gold bars floated up and away. Lando grabbed them before he realized what they were. Gold bars! Holy Sol! He was rich!

Cramming the bars back inside the satchel, Lando saw more, ten or twelve more, each stamped with the Imperial seal.

And then the joy was gone. "Now wait a minute," a voice said. "That's Imperial gold in that satchel. You know, the kind that belongs to the Emperor, the kind he wants back. Take it, and you'll be lucky to end up on a prison planet."

Lando felt sure that another part of his personality had an adequate response but he never got to hear it.

"Your read me, Pik?" Melissa's voice was tense.

"Loud and clear."

"There's a ship coming our way. She's ignoring the beacons and my calls."

Lando swore softly and snapped the satchel to his chest. The stiff could wait. He opened the gate, secured it behind him, and unhooked the lifeline from the mesh. Snapping the hook onto a fitting located just behind his neck, Lando saw a green light come on above his visor, and kicked off.

"Melissa, I'm on my way. Keep trying to raise the other ship."

"That's a roger." She sounded better now that he was on the way.

Lando fired his suit jets and aimed for the black triangle located between the tender's navigational lights.

"Pik!" Melissa sounded scared. "The ship's picking up speed! It's coming toward you!"

Lando turned and tried to locate the oncoming ship's navigational lights. There weren't any. A rock fell straight to the pit of his stomach. No com, no lights, the bastards were trying to run him down!

"Reel me in, Melissa! Do it now!"

Melissa obeyed and Lando felt himself jerked backward. He wasn't sure which was faster, his suit jets or the electric winch, but he couldn't stand the idea of being hit from behind. At least this way he'd see it coming.

And there it was. The sun had risen relative to Lando, and it backlit the ship, making it appear black and menacing.

Lando was momentarily blinded by a pulse of blue light. An energy cannon! The bastards were shooting at him, or the tender, he couldn't tell which.

Seconds passed while Lando waited to die. Nothing happened. That was good . . . but something was wrong. Then he had it. The pull of the emergency line had disappeared. The sonsabitches had cut him loose!

Lando fired his suit jets but moved too late. Something locked on to him with crushing force. He blacked out and came to seconds later.

"Pik! Pik! What's going on?" Melissa was terrified.

Lando tried to speak but found he couldn't. It took every erg of energy he had to breathe. His eyes told him that the black ship was moving closer. What the hell were they doing to him? Then he understood. A tractor beam. The miserable bastards had speared him with a tractor beam. But why?

His first thought was the gold but he quickly dismissed that. There was no way they could know about the gold. No, it must be something else, something . . .

The pressure suddenly disappeared. Lando was floating in space.

"Well, well," a voice said. "Look at that. A piece of space junk. People are *so* rude. They leave their garbage all over the place. What if we hit it? That space armor could scratch our paint job!

"No, our duty is clear. A clean orbit is a safe orbit. Wouldn't you agree, Citizen Lando? That's your name, isn't it? It's the one dear old Cap listed on the contract with Pylax."

"Screw you, Willer."

"Such unpleasant language," Willer observed mockingly. "Still, if it makes you feel better, I'm willing to listen. Any last words?"

Lando forced a chuckle. "Yeah, chrome dork, how're your knees?"

An invisible club came out of nowhere and blasted Lando into space.

As G's piled on top of G's, a big black hand reached up to pull Lando down. Well I'll be damned, Lando thought to himself, death isn't so bad after all.

7

Cap stepped out of the bank and looked around. Pylax was very different from Dista. In place of muddy trails there were broad well-paved streets packed with bumper-to-bumper traffic. Horns beeped, loud music leaked out of stores, sirens wailed, and well-dressed people made a swirl of color.

Cap smiled, sidestepped an intense young man with a shiny portacomp, and looked for a place to relax. Retail shops, restaurants, and lounges occupied the first two floors of every building in sight. Signs pulsated, flashed, and glowed. There were bars aplenty. There were upscale bars, downscale bars, and ethnic bars but none that catered to spacers.

Cap held up a hand and jumped in the backseat when an auto cab whirred to the curb. "Your destination please?"

"Blast Town. Give me a bar patronized by spacers."

The cab whirred away from the curb. "There are a number of good bars located adjacent to the port. I have paid advertisements for three of them."

"Play back please."

Cap listened as the auto cab played them back. All three sounded fine, but Cap chose Blaster Willie's, since it was the oldest. It was his experience that older bars have more flavor, more tradition, and more interesting clientele. Besides, Willie's was closest to the port, and therefore most convenient.

As the downtown section of Brisco City disappeared behind him, Cap saw more and more warehouses, until they gave way to the bars and brothels of Blast Town.

Blast Town. A place he'd have avoided like the plague in the old days, the days when he was one of the Empire Line's most promising young officers, and snotty as hell. Back then he looked down on people who drank cheap booze in smelly bars. Back then he was very young.

The auto cab pulled to the curb, accepted Cap's fare, and thanked him for the business. Willie's had a holo sign, a three-dimensional affair, in which a horizontal whiskey bottle poured electronic booze into an equally horizontal shot glass.

Glancing around, Cap saw that the other bars had equally fanciful facades, suggesting a competition to see which establishment could come up with the most garish sign of all.

Once inside Willie's it was dark, dirty, and completely satisfactory. Cap licked his lips as he stepped up to the bar and ordered a drink.

The barkeep wore an eye patch made out of something or somebody with green scaly skin. His apron was so dirty that Cap couldn't discern its original color. "One whiskey comin' up, sir. You wanta pay or run a tab?"

"I think I'll run a tab," Cap replied. It would call for exquisite judgment but if he drank just the right amount he could get reasonably sloshed and still fly the speedster. It was only a short hop into orbit and one rotation home.

He looked around. Willie's was nearly empty. "Not much business today."

The barkeep shrugged and wiped the countertop with a wet rag. "Well, sir, it's early yet. On toward nighttime we start to fill up."

Cap nodded. "Where's the men's room?"

"Right over there," the bartender replied, pointing across the room. "Take a right at the roid miner."

"Roid miner?" Cap squinted into the dark.

Sure enough, a woman dressed in a set of beat-up leathers sat slumped in a chair, her back to the bar. Maybe she knew something interesting, maybe not. A drink was a small price to pay to find out.

Besides, talking with her would justify his presence in the bar, and elevate his drinking to the category of "business research."

Cap signaled the barkeep and pointed to the miner. "Give her another of whatever she's drinking."

The bartender gave Cap a knowing grin and reached for another glass.

By the time Cap returned from the men's room, his drink and a tall glass of green liquor sat in front of the miner.

She wore her hair high and tight marine style. She had a broad forehead, an upturned nose, and a no-nonsense mouth. The telltale rub burns on her forehead and cheeks hinted at endless hours spent in space armor. A roid miner for sure.

"I don't screw for drinks, mister. So if that's the plan, then forget it."

Cap smiled. "No plan, and other than some conversation, no obligation."

The woman nodded. "Fair enough. Just thought you should know. Have a seat. My name's Libby Nox. Most people just call me Nox, or Noxie."

"All right, Noxie. My name's Sorenson. People call me Cap. What brings you to Pylax?"

In his efforts to locate the *Star of Empire* Cap had conducted hundreds, maybe even thousands of similar interviews over the last few years, and the first part of Noxie's story was quite typical.

According to Noxie she and her partner, a woman named Farley, had worked a claim deep in the belt. Things were tough, but the two women made do, even scratched out a small profit until their claim took a direct hit from a "buster."

"Busters" were large chunks of rock that careened from asteroid to asteroid like enormous cue balls, knocking them out of their established orbits, and "busting" the small ones into even smaller pieces. Such was the fate of Noxie's claim.

Fortunately for her, Noxie was away at the time, using their scooter to scout another rock. Farley wasn't so lucky. She along with their small ship disappeared during the moment of impact.

Like most roid miners the two women had established an emergency supply dump on a nearby asteroid. Included was enough oxygen, food, and water to make it out of the belt. Loading it aboard a sled, and hooking the sled to her scooter, Noxie began the long arduous journey to the nearest gate. Once there she could take shelter in a dome provided for that purpose, activate an emergency beacon, and wait for help.

While incredible, the story up to this point was far from unusual, the rigors of the belt being what they were. But then, well lubricated by her fourth drink, Noxie said something that pushed the alcohol out of Cap's brain.

"Yeah," Noxie said, "strangely enough the O_2 was holding out, but my food was running low, and ditto the water. So there I was, getting ready to make the big jump, when I seen this ship."

"A ship?"

"That's what I said isn't it? A ship. A big sucker, big enough to be a liner, you know the kind I mean?"

"Yes," Cap answered excitedly. "I know the kind you mean. What happened next?"

"Well," Noxie said, more than a little drunk, "I thought my ass was saved. I thought they'd take me aboard, buy me dinner, and show me to a stateroom."

"And?" Cap asked, sensing where Noxie was going, and impatient to get there.

"And it was a drifter," Noxie answered dramatically. "A ghost ship. I was shit out of luck."

"Did you board her?"

Noxie shook her head. "No time. I was short on supplies remember? And it was spooky. No, I hauled butt."

"What did she look like?" Cap asked eagerly. "Can you describe her?"

Noxie finished a drink and wiped her nose with the back of her sleeve. "Why bother? Ain't a picture worth a thousand words?"

"You took a picture?" Cap asked, his heart in his throat. My God, after all these years, what if it was the *Star of Empire*?

"Hell yes," Noxie replied, fumbling around inside her jacket. "I've got it here someplace, wait a minute, here. Take a look at that."

As Cap took the crumpled holopix his hands trembled. Fighting back the effects of alcohol, Cap forced his eyes to focus and gave a grunt of satisfaction.

It was a ship all right, a big one, big enough to be the *Star of Empire*.

Unfortunately the picture was slightly out of focus. Just enough to prevent absolute identification, but what the hell, given the vessel's size and shape it had to be the *Empire*.

She was out there! Relatively undamaged and waiting for him to find her!

There was a tremble in Cap's voice as he asked the next question. "It looks interesting, Noxie, real interesting, a drifter sure enough. I don't suppose you took some bearings?"

A crafty look came over Noxie's face and Cap found himself wondering just how drunk she really was. "Suppose I did?

"Information like that would be worth money, lots of money, especially to someone in the salvage business. And that's you, isn't it, Cap? You're in the salvage business. In fact, I'll bet that you're captain of a salvage tug, and that's why they call you Cap."

Cap made no effort to deny it. Negotiations began. They lasted for the better part of an hour. Cap found Noxie to be a shrewd negotiator and nobody's fool. She knew Cap wanted the drifter, and wanted it bad. And having lost everything to the buster, she was determined to get everything she could.

So when the two of them shook hands Cap was broke. Noxie had all his money. She had *Junk*'s operating budget for the next two months, electronically transferred from his account to hers, *plus* the crew's pay.

Cap felt sure they'd understand, and even if they didn't, he'd sweet-talk them into waiting a bit longer. After all, they knew he was a drunk, and drunks do irresponsible things.

So it was with a sense of triumph that Cap zipped the bearings into the inside pocket of his coat, hoisted one last drink with Noxie, and set out for the spaceport.

There was a spring in his step as he passed through the gates. He'd done a good piece of business, the *Star of Empire* was out there waiting for him, and he could still walk without assistance. Mel would be proud.

All landing fees were paid cash in advance, so it was a simple matter to wave his plastic receipt at a scanner, and make his way out onto the field. Lacking the money for a ground shuttle he walked toward the speedster.

It was about two miles out to the low-cost landing grids and the sun was hot. The combination of the heat and the alcohol made Cap's head swim.

The walk seemed to last forever, but finally he was there, climbing into the cockpit and entering his code.

The moment Cap hit the last digit a beeper went off accompanied by a flashing red light. There was a message waiting.

What now? Couldn't it wait until he came aboard?

Cap pressed a button, heard a moment of static, followed by Melissa's voice. His daughter's obvious desperation sobered Cap up faster than a bucket of cold water.

"Daddy! Pik was outside working in the trap. Willer came and did something horrible to him. Cy's got *Junk*'s control system torn apart and it'll be half an hour before he gets it back together.

"Cy says help's on the way, but I'm afraid they'll take too long, so I'm going after Pik myself. Daddy, I need your help, but if you're sick, don't try to take off."

Cap swore, bypassed the normal start-up procedures, and went for emergency lift. The control tower was still screaming threats as the speedster screamed over the horizon and climbed toward space.

As heavy G's crushed Cap's chest and drove the blood from his brain, he could still hear her words: "Daddy, I need your help, but if you're sick, don't try to take off." Shame rolled over him like a wave and he cursed his own weakness.

Melissa bit her lip until blood came. What looked so easy when Lando did it was almost impossible for her. The tender seemed huge and awkward under her hands. It wallowed through turns, drifted to port and starboard, and punished her with flashing red lights. There were so many things to do, so many things to remember, and underlying it all the incessant tone from Lando's locator beacon.

Melissa couldn't tell whether Lando was alive or dead, but his suit was functioning, and that gave her hope. She wasn't sure what Willer had done to Lando, but given the way the pilot's suit had accelerated out and away from the tender, it seemed as if the cyborg had clobbered him with a pressor beam.

Melissa tried to imagine what that would feel like. To be hit with a club so powerful it could move battleships, to be hurled into space, to be all alone.

Melissa shuddered. Well, she'd find him. She'd follow the locator signal to its source, get him into the lock, and . . . Tears began to flow.

What if Lando were dead? What if she'd killed him the same way she'd killed Lia? The thought was unbearable.

The tone was louder now, indicating she was closer. She could see it on the scanner screen, a flashing light that indicated electronic emissions, and a dwindling set of digits.

Melissa fumbled with the controls, started to fire retros, and remembered to dump power first. There . . . no, still too fast . . . fire the retros again.

Melissa's hair was wet with sweat as the tender slowed and matched speeds with Lando's suit. She'd done it! Releasing her harness, Melissa rolled up and out of her seat. Grabbing handholds, she raced for the lock.

A buzzer went off. Melissa stopped. The buzzer was part of the ship but the voice in her head belonged to Lando.

"A pilot never . . . repeat never . . . leaves the board without running a NAVCOMP sequence. There are three programs to choose from: auto run, auto standby, and auto shutdown. Each program . . ."

Melissa gave a little cry of frustration.

She turned, pulled herself back to the control room, and tapped some instructions into the NAVCOMP. The buzzer stopped, the tender's drive and control systems went over to standby, and Melissa heaved a sigh of relief. She gave a powerful kick and headed for the lock.

Melissa had considered using the tractor-pressor beams to reach out and grab Lando but she was afraid to try. One little mistake and she could push him beyond reach or smash him against the hull. No, it was simpler and safer to suit-up and go after Lando in person.

With her suit sealed Melissa waited for the outer hatch to cycle open and tried her radio. "Pik . . . this is Melissa. Do you read me, Pik?"

No answer.

The circular hatch was only half-dilated when Melissa dived through. Pylax floated like an amber-colored jewel against the black velvet of space.

But Melissa ignored the planet and everything beyond to concentrate her attention on a single point of reflected light, the steady tone that emanated from it, and the actions necessary to reach it.

Suddenly all hesitation was gone. Space was Melissa's element, her playground, the place where she'd grown up. She'd been going outside for five years now, and even Cap said she was good, better than most grown-ups.

Melissa fired her suit jets in a long steady burst of power, watched the gleam of light turn into a space suit, and did a half somersault. She waited for the jets to slow her down, cut power at just the right moment, and threw her arms around Lando's left leg.

Melissa wasn't a bit surprised at her success. Only impatient to reach the tender, scared of what she might find when she got there, and worried about her ability to handle it.

What if Lando needed emergency medical attention? What if she had to dock with a habitat or, Sol forbid, land on Pylax? Could she do it?

These questions and others plagued Melissa as she grabbed onto Lando's external power pak and blasted for the tender. It was awkward, but Melissa had handled large loads many times before, and this wasn't much different. Lando's external air gauge was in the red so speed was of the essence.

The little ship came up quickly, and Melissa gave thanks for zero G, as she followed Lando's inert form through the hatch and cycled the lock.

Pushing Lando over to a suit lock Melissa engaged the electromagnet and did the same for herself. After that it was a matter of listening to the pulse pound in her head and waiting for the lock to pressurize.

Finally, after what seemed an eternity, the green light came on and Melissa could break her seals.

Pulling herself over to Lando, Melissa tried to see through his visor and failed.

"Pik? Can you hear me? It's Melissa. I'm opening your suit, Pik. Oh, please, Pik, say something, anything. Tell me you're okay. I promise I'll be good. I'll learn all the math the auto tutor can teach me, I'll clean my cabin twice a week, and I'll wet vac the hydroponics tank without being asked. Please, Pik . . . wake up."

Melissa pulled his helmet off and saw that he was breathing. Thank God! His eyelids fluttered and popped open. Slowly, very slowly, Lando's eyes came into focus. His voice was little more than a croak.

"You promise?"

"Pik . . . I'll get some help . . ."

"You promise about the math?"

"Sure . . . listen, Pik . . ."

"Say it."

"I promise to do my math."

"Good girl," Lando replied with just the trace of a smile. "Now drag whatever's left of my body to a bunk and strap it in. I need a nap."

8

Lando looked in the mirror and winced. His face was black and blue. Even though a complete medical examination had failed to turn up any broken bones or internal injuries, the pressor beam had ruptured thousands of capillaries just under the skin and turned Lando's body into a giant bruise.

In fact, the doctor Cap had flown up from Pylax had pronounced him "lucky to be alive," and had shaken her head in amazement.

Lando agreed. He *was* lucky to be alive. Lucky there'd been plenty of open space behind him, and lucky that Melissa had come after him before his suit ran out of air.

Lando remembered the fear in her voice, the pale little face, and the joy when he spoke. He smiled and it hurt.

Fumbling around in the medicine cabinet, Lando found a couple of pain tabs, placed them on his tongue, and chased them with some water.

The doctor had suggested a zero-G environment for his convalescence, but Lando had refused, pointing out that the movements required during weightlessness would hurt just as much or more. Besides, this way he could sleep in his own cabin, and that felt good.

The intercom bonged gently over his head.

"Yeah?"

"How're you feeling?" The voice belonged to Cap. A day late and a credit short as always, but very solicitous.

Especially after informing Cy and Lando that he'd used *their* salaries to buy coordinates for what *might,* or *might not,* be the

Star of Empire, based on a fuzzy photo obtained from a woman in a bar.

It was pure Cap, or crap, depending how you viewed it, and Lando was pissed. But in his present condition the pilot was too beat-up to do more than grit his teeth and go along. "I feel even worse than I look."

"Sorry to hear that," Cap replied, doing his very best to sound sincere.

"Would you know anything about a dead body? We just got a com call from some naval lieutenant. A guy called Itek. He's looking for an Imperial Courier. A man named Nugleo. According to the lieutenant this Nugleo guy turned up missing three or four weeks ago, and for reasons that aren't clear could be orbiting Pylax in a space suit.

"I told him no, we didn't know anything about it, but Mel says you found a body. True?"

All sorts of thoughts raced through Lando's mind. The bounty on his head, the dead body wired to the inside of the trap, and the gold-filled satchel.

Great Sol! The gold! Where was it? Still connected to his suit? Lando hobbled toward the door. "This lieutenant . . . where is he?"

"On his way up from Pylax," Cap answered curiously. "Why? Is that a problem?"

"It might be," Lando answered tightly. "Meet me at the tender."

Fifteen minutes later Lando opened the tender's lock while Cap looked on. The older man wanted to ask a lot of questions but something about the expression on Lando's face kept him from doing so.

The space suit was right where he'd left it, and yes, the satchel was still in place.

Lando unsnapped the satchel and its sudden weight jerked his hand toward the deck. Wincing at the effort, Lando carried the bag to the outer hatch and dropped it into Cap's waiting arms.

Cap staggered, recovered, and did a double take when he saw the Imperial crest that was woven into the satchel's fabric. "What the . . . ?"

"Take a look inside," Lando answered impassively. "I think you'll find the contents rather interesting."

Cap fumbled the satchel open and looked inside. Lando smiled at the look of pure unadulterated avarice that came over the other man's face. "That's right . . . gold. Enough gold to keep all of us happy for the next year or so."

Cap looked up. "The courier? You didn't . . ."

"Don't be silly," Lando replied scornfully. "The courier had been missing for weeks, remember? No, I didn't kill him, I found him, that's all. He was drifting around Pylax with all the other junk. And that means the gold is ours, right?"

Cap frowned and hefted the satchel with his right hand. "I don't know, Lando . . . our contract gives us salvage rights to whatever we find . . . that's true enough. But Imperial gold? Chances are it's covered in the fine print."

Lando swore softly as he climbed down and rubbed the back of his neck. Like the rest of his body it hurt. Cap was probably right. It was just like his father had always said: "Governments are all the same, son, they take most of what you make and spend it on themselves."

Lando cleared his throat. "That being the case . . . maybe we should forget the gold. You know, stash it somewhere. After all, somebody killed the courier, that's clear, and your lieutenant will assume *they* took the gold."

Cap forced his eyes up and away from the gold. "Killed? Why do you say that?"

"Somebody drilled him with an energy weapon," Lando replied patiently. "He was wearing one of those top-end self-sealing suits, but the bolt went clear through, and that made him extremely dead."

The intercom bonged over their heads. The voice belonged to Cy. "Cap, a navy shuttle just came alongside, and a Lieutenant Itek requests permission to come aboard."

There was a long moment of silence during which nothing was said but the two men continued to look each other in the eye.

Cap was the first to speak. "All right, Lando . . . let's stash the gold and hope for the best. You've got the body?"

"It's inside the trap."

Cap nodded and yelled toward the overhead. "Okay, Cy. Give us a moment to get clear, tell Itek to come aboard, and depressurize the bay. We'll meet him when he clears the lock."

"That's a roger," Cy answered crisply, and clicked off.

Forty minutes later the gold was safely hidden, Cap and Lando had phony smiles plastered across their faces, and Lieutenant Itek was stepping out of the lock.

He was short as naval types go, about five feet five or six, but athletic in a low blocky way. Itek's space black uniform hugged his considerable muscles and suggested a good tailor. He had short sandy hair, a nose that was a little too large for the rest of his face, and intelligent brown eyes. *Extremely* intelligent brown eyes. So much so that Lando felt his heart sink as he shook the other man's hand.

"Pik Lando, Lieutenant, and this is Cap Sorenson."

Itek smiled. "It's a pleasure, gentlemen. Sorry to take your valuable time, but the Emp gets rather protective when it comes to his couriers, and it happens that one is missing. Interesting ship, Captain . . . a custom design?"

Cap replied that it was, and as he led Itek toward the cabin that he used as an office, he proceeded to describe *Junk*'s dubious merits.

Lando had a bad feeling as he followed along behind. For all his casual chatter, and flip references to the Emperor, Lieutenant Itek was no fool. Quite the opposite. Under the friendly surface Lando sensed an agile mind and a heart of pure steel. And unless Lando missed his guess, they were in deep trouble.

Cap's office showed signs of a recent cleanup, Melissa's doing no doubt, and the three men were able to sit down without clearing stuff off their chairs. The piles of printouts, worn-out ship parts, and keepsakes from Cap's more memorable tows were still present but neatly stacked. If the ship's argrav shut down, it would take years to collect the stuff and get it under control.

Doing his best to look relaxed and confident, Cap leaned back in his chair and clasped both hands over his stomach.

"We're glad you came, Lieutenant. As it happens we *do* know something about the missing courier. Unbeknownst to me, Lando here found him, and was on his way back to our tender, when parties unknown hit him with a pressor beam. Well, that put Lando out of commission for a while, so he couldn't tell me about the body. I heard about it a few minutes ago."

Itek raised an eyebrow. "Excellent! The search is over. Body you say. Poor Nugleo. The Emp will be quite upset. Any signs of foul play?"

Lando nodded. No doubt about it. Itek was a dangerous man. The naval officer was way ahead of them. Lando felt a trickle of sweat run down his spine.

"I'm afraid so, Lieutenant. The light was poor, but it appeared as if Nugleo had been hit with some sort of energy weapon. Whatever it was went straight through and out the other side."

Itek nodded as if expecting to hear something of the sort. "And the location of the body?"

"It's inside the trap. As Cap indicated I was on my way for help when somebody gave me a love tap with a pressor beam."

Itek pulled a communicator off his belt and spoke into it. "Ensign Davison, do you read me?"

"Loud and clear, Lieutenant."

"Keep an eye on item Tango. No one in or out without my permission."

Davison answered, "Aye, aye, sir," and clicked off.

Lando felt the trickle of sweat that ran down his back become a river. Itek had provided himself with a backup, a backup that was close enough to watch the trap. Now why would the naval officer do that unless he was suspicious?

Itek returned the communicator to his belt. "Sorry about the pressor beam, Citizen Lando . . . you're lucky to be alive. Parties unknown? A bit unusual, don't you think?"

There was just the hint of a smile around Itek's mouth as he spoke, as if to say that they could claim whatever they wanted, but he wouldn't believe it.

The truth was that Cap wanted to report Willer, but they had no proof, and without it the accusation would do little more than cause more trouble. All Melissa could do was testify that a darkened ship had passed through the area, that someone who sounded like Jord Willer had made threatening comments, and presumably hit Lando with a pressor beam.

Lando shrugged. "*Very* unusual. And *very* unpleasant."

"Yes," Itek agreed. "I'm sure it was. Well, enough of that. There's another matter to discuss however . . . and that's the satchel that Nugleo wore prior to his death."

Lando started to speak but stopped when Itek held up a well-manicured hand. "Please, Citizen Lando, let me finish. You'll be glad you did. Even seen one of these before?"

Lando stared at the little black box that the naval officer had removed from his breast pocket. He knew exactly what it was, and a single glance told him that Cap did too. Still, there was no point in admitting any more than he had to. When he spoke Lando's voice was a croak. "I don't think so . . . what is it?"

"A low-powered detector," Itek answered conversationally. "It doesn't have much range, but when it gets within a few hundred yards of the proper transmitter, this light blinks on and off."

Cap stared at the ruby red light as if transfixed.

"The really interesting part," Itek continued calmly, "is that the transmitter's woven into the fabric of the satchel that Courier Nugleo carried, and it's somewhere aboard this ship."

A moment of silence passed before Cap cleared his throat. "Yes, well, I, that is, we were going to mention that. I didn't want to say anything over the air lest the wrong ears hear, but when Lando discovered Nugleo, he fastened the satchel to his suit for safekeeping. I'll go get it."

Itek held up a hand. "That won't be necessary, at least not yet, and maybe never. You're businessmen . . . so let's discuss some business."

Cap sat back in his seat and Lando paid close attention. As his fear began to disappear it was replaced by a growing sense of excitement. There was a deal in the offing, a deal in which they could keep the gold! Now for the price.

Itek looked at Lando and smiled. "Here's the situation. Assume that Courier Nugleo was less than perfect. More than that . . . assume Nugleo fell in with bad company. A woman named Leslie Corbin to be precise, and that she taught him to do naughty things, like steal gold from the Emperor."

Lando swallowed and forced a smile. By now his entire body was bathed in sweat.

"Not that poor old Nugleo thought he was *stealing* the gold," Itek continued softly. "Oh, no. By the time Corbin was finished, Nugleo believed that the government *owed* him the gold, in return for his many years of outstanding service.

"So the two of them hatched a plan," Itek said, staring off into space as if he could actually see it. "The plan involved using the gold to buy some drugs, yirl to be exact, and selling it for an enormous profit. Enough to live on for the rest of their lives."

Itek looked down, first at Cap, then at Lando. "It didn't work. Corbin used her connections with the underworld to set up a buy. For days they sat next to a comset and waited. When the call came they were given two hours to make a meeting in space. They blasted off in Nugleo's official speedster, found the right ship, and landed in a huge bay.

"They took a look around, but outside of the two men waiting to greet them, the bay was empty. They climbed out of the speedster."

Having participated in similar meetings himself, Lando could imagine what it was like. The knot of fear in your stomach, the bright green cargo lights, and the sound of your own breathing inside the suit.

"The bay was unpressurized," Itek continued, "so Nugleo and Corbin stayed in their suits. Negotiations got under way, and things were going well, until time came to exchange gold for drugs. Suddenly all hell broke loose.

"Five or six men dropped down from up above. Nugleo nailed one, Corbin another. Nugleo took a bolt through the abdomen. Corbin grabbed him and dragged him toward the speedster. In the meantime energy bolts were flying every which way."

Itek smiled cynically. "It's hard to say whether Corbin was trying to save Nugleo or the gold. She claims it was Nugleo, I think it was the gold. In any case, Corbin saw that the speedster was hopeless, so she did the next best thing. She jumped out of the open hatch with Nugleo in tow. As Corbin cleared the ship's argrav and hit zero G she fired her suit jets and was gone."

Was there a trace of admiration in the way Itek told the story? Lando thought so, but couldn't be sure.

Itek shrugged. "From there it's somewhat obvious. The drug runners gave chase, Corbin gave them the slip, but lost Nugleo in the process. When her air ran low, Corbin activated her emergency suit beacon, and as luck would have it, a navy shuttle got to her before the smugglers could.

"Suffice it to say that we asked her a lot of questions, and in the long run, she gave us a lot of answers. We'd spent two weeks searching for Nugleo's body by the time I heard about your orbital cleanup contract, and the rest is, as they say, 'history'."

"That's all very interesting," Cap said, "but I fail to see how it impacts us. You said something about a business proposition."

"Correct," Itek agreed cheerfully. "I'm coming to that. First, however, you must understand that the Emperor has an iron-clad policy regarding his couriers. It goes something like this, 'Touch them and you die.' "

Itek looked from one man to the other. "Yes, even if the courier does something criminal. You see, given the fact that science has yet to bless us with some sort of faster-than-light radio, and given the fact that the Emperor's dispatches travel by courier, he insists they be absolutely untouchable. That's why he ordered the navy to find Nugleo's killers and bring them in."

"Or?" Lando asked, knowing the answer.

"Or kill them," Itek answered easily, "and that's where *you* come in."

Cap ran his tongue over dry lips. He forced a smile. "Where we come in? I don't understand."

Itek smiled. "Not you, just Citizen Lando here, crack pilot and smuggler extraordinaire."

"Smuggler?" Cap looked from Itek to Lando.

"Ooops!" Itek held a hand to his mouth in mock chagrin. "Did I let the secret out? Did Citizen Lando forget to mention smuggling on his résumé? How embarrassing!"

Lando shrugged in answer to Cap's unasked question. "Yeah, I used to run some of this and that, it was no big deal."

Itek shook his head in mock concern. "Citizen Lando is far too modest. The truth is that he's wanted for murder. I know, because I ran a routine background check on your entire crew just before I left Pylax."

"It wasn't murder," Lando said stubbornly. "It was self-defense. My father bribed a customs inspector to look the other way. When we landed the inspector killed my father in cold blood. I evened the score."

Itek smiled patiently. "Whatever. It makes little difference to me. With the exception of cases like Nugleo, the navy doesn't enforce civil law."

"Well, it makes a difference to me!" Cap said angrily. "Lando, you're fired!"

"Whoa," Itek said, holding up a hand in protest. "I said a 'business' deal, remember? And Citizen Lando is an important part of the deal."

Lando ignored Cap. "Tell us about this 'deal' of yours."

Itek grinned. "I thought you'd never ask! It works like this: Corbin knows where the killers are, or thinks she does. We go there, arrest 'em, and bring 'em back."

"And if they don't want to come?"

Itek shrugged. "We shoot 'em."

"Well, the plan is certainly straightforward," Lando said dryly. "But why me? What you need is a squad of marines."

"That would be nice," Itek agreed, "but a squad of marines can't get me onto Devo's Disk. That takes a one-hundred-percent-pure dyed-in-the-wool criminal, and that's you."

Lando thought it over. He didn't care for the word "criminal" but Itek was right nonetheless. Nobody got aboard the space habitat known as Devo's Disk without the recommendation of a known criminal. And much as he hated to admit it, Lando fit the bill. He'd been there many times over the years, both with and without his father, and would have no trouble getting aboard. And based on his recommendation, they would accept Itek as well.

Yes, getting aboard would be easy. Getting off, well, that would be a problem. Especially with one or more prisoners in tow or, if worse came to worst, a firefight raging around them. Still, given Itek's none-too-subtle threats, he didn't have a whole lot of choice.

"I go and the gold is ours?"

Itek smiled. "That's right. And I forget we ever met."

Lando looked at Cap. "I get my back wages, plus a full share of the gold, plus I stay aboard as long as I want to."

Cap glowered, started to say something, and nodded instead. "Right."

"Good. Okay, Lieutenant, I sure hope you're a lucky man, 'cause we're gonna need all the luck you've got and then some."

9

Sunlight glittered off the space station's alloy hull so that Devo's Disk hung like a golden crown against the blackness of space. Its multicolored navigational lights sparkled like precious gems, the forest of antennae that circled the habitat's outer edge looked like gold filigree, and the mile-long rail gun that floated nearby had the appearance of a silver scepter.

Once, hundreds of years before, the disk had carried settlers to their new homes among the stars. But that was long ago, and now it had a different purpose.

Now it was home to thieves, smugglers, and worse.

And rumor had it that pirate ships stopped there as well, not the ragtag collection of bandits who plagued the asteroids, but the *real* thing.

Men and women who fought for the Confederation and lost, or were born to those who had, and made a precarious living raiding the frontier worlds.

In the beginning they were soldiers, defenders of a crumbling democracy, patriots who believed in a noble cause. They fought battle after battle but in the long run lost the war. Most surrendered, accepted the generous terms offered by the newly proclaimed Emperor, and turned their attention to war-ravaged planets.

But some refused to quit, vowed to fight on, and did so. Over time, however, idealism had given way to self-centered pragmatism and left them little more than thieves.

Powerful thieves, however, since the pirates had their own planet and other haunts as well, Devo's Disk being one of them.

Lando checked his readouts and cut the scout ship's speed. It was a handy little vessel, incredibly fast, and better armed than one might think.

Having entered hyperspace off Durna, the scout exited three days later near Eron IV, and headed in-system. This was where Lando had been born and spent his younger days. It was also the system in which his father had died and he was wanted for murder. A fact that took any pleasure from his return.

Impatient to get the trip over and return, Lando pushed the ship hard, racing away from Eron IV's fiery shape, and toward the darkness of the frontier. And there, hovering between the human empire and the dark unknown, was Devo's Disk.

The location was no accident. Following the example of countless merchants before him, Devo had positioned his business next to an important trade route, and thereby gained an advantage over most of his competition.

Positioned as he was, halfway between Eron IV's developed planets and the frontier, Devo bought rim goods low and sold manufactured goods high. People complained, but Devo had a standard reply:

"You want a better price for your grain? Fine. Go ahead. Spend the next week traveling in-system. The inner planets will pay you more . . . and get it back when you buy their fuel!"

When convenient, Devo gave the opposite argument as well.

"You want more money for your robo-reapers? Great. Take 'em out along the rim and sell 'em yourself. Assuming that the pirates don't steal your cargo, and the Il Ronn don't use your ship for target practice, the settlers will pay you more. Good luck."

That was the honest and aboveboard part of Devo's business. But there was another part as well. Due to its location the Disk was also the perfect place to broker drug shipments, buy stolen goods, and sell supplies to the pirates.

Yes, Lando reflected, it was a good location indeed. He yawned.

The trip had been relatively quick, but even so, the better part of a week had passed since breaking orbit off Pylax and Lando was tired. Tired of Itek's superior attitude, tired of a trip he didn't want to take, and tired of the tiny ship. There was barely enough room for Lando, Itek, and Martinez to sit in the control area all at once.

Martinez was a pilot, a rather hot pilot according to Itek, although she didn't look it. At the moment she was slouched in the co-pilot's position, apparently half-asleep, humming to herself.

She had short black hair, little-girl features, and a skinny body. It was warm inside the small ship and Martinez was dressed in regulation blue shorts and halter top. Lando noticed a small tattoo on her left shoulder. A skull and crossbones. Weird. Like everything else on this trip Martinez was a mystery, a piece of the puzzle, a part of Itek's master plan.

With Lando and Martinez sitting up front, Itek was crammed into a jump seat located slightly to the rear.

"Why the cut in speed?" the naval officer inquired, looking up from the holo reader on his lap.

"So they don't blow us into the next galaxy," Lando answered, crossly pointing up at the main screen. "Take a look at that rail gun."

Itek looked at the main screen and saw that the silver scepter had changed position. It was now pointed in their direction.

"So that's a rail gun," Martinez said lazily. "A little outdated, isn't it?"

Lando shrugged. She sounded superior and he didn't like it. "A lot outdated, and far from the only weapons pointed our way, but that's Devo for you. He likes old stuff. Last time I saw him he was packing a pair of antique slug throwers. They were at least a thousand years old, but they worked, and they could still blow your head off."

"The philosopher has spoken," Itek said sarcastically. "And having done so, has time to answer that incoming com call."

Lando glanced at the control board, saw the flashing red light, and touched a screen. Two words were revealed as it faded up from black: "ENTER CODE."

The smuggler bit his lip. Once he entered the code it would change the rest of his life. By entering his personal code, then violating Devo's covenants, Lando would ban himself from his father's world. A world of corruption, theft, and worse, but one he understood.

And for what? Honest citizens would still avoid him, bounty hunters would still search for him, and he'd be stuck in between. Not criminal, not in his mind anyway, and not honest citizen either. It seemed that ever since his father's death he'd been on the run, not just from one world, but from both.

Itek cleared his throat impatiently and Lando typed in the code. It was a long string of apparently meaningless letters and numbers. He'd complained when his father had asked him to memorize it and been told to shut up and do it anyway.

When Lando was done, the words "HOLD PLEASE . . ." flashed on the screen, while Devo's computers checked his entry for authenticity. A fraction of a second later those words disappeared and were replaced by: "WELCOME, PIK LANDO, YOU MAY APPROACH," followed by a graphic display.

Itek nodded in approval. "Well done. It appears you're a criminal in good standing. Martinez will take it from here."

The sleepy look disappeared as Martinez sat straight up, glanced at the com screen, and took over the controls. Judging from the smooth way in which Martinez slid the scout into their assigned approach vector, the young woman knew what she was doing.

"Come on, Lando, it's show time." Without waiting for a response Itek released his harness and propelled himself toward the vessel's tiny lounge. Like most navy scouts this one came unencumbered by niceties like argrav generators.

By the time Lando reached the lounge Itek had already hooked himself to a bulkhead. "Lock on. We need to rehearse our plan."

"Why bother?" Lando inquired, backing into one of the four padded positions. "Why not slag the disk and be done with it? A battlewagon could do the job in half an hour, rail gun or no rail gun."

"What?" Itek asked in mock concern. "Kill hundreds of possibly innocent men, women, and children just to get the two we want? I'm shocked."

"No you aren't," Lando said stubbornly. "The navy does worse all the time. There's another reason, isn't there?"

Itek nodded approvingly. "Excellent. You *can* think. Yes, there's another reason, a good one. Our goal is to use these people as an example, to deter others, to prove we have teeth."

"So you *need* witnesses," Lando mused. "There's a problem though. A rather large one. Once we find the killers how do we get them off the disk? There are two locks, and no matter which one we use, the guards will stop us. End of story."

"I anticipated that," Itek answered calmly. "We'll avoid the locks."

"Avoid them?" Lando demanded. "How?"

"Simple," Itek answered. "We'll use explosives to make a *new* hatch."

"But that will kill everyone aboard!"

"Not if we seal the compartment off first," Itek replied patiently. "Then it's a simple matter of making the hole, stepping outside, and waiting for Martinez to pick us up."

"That's just wonderful," Lando said sarcastically. "Except for one thing. Devo's security team won't allow us to bring the explosives on board, or weapons either!"

"Oh, yes, they will," Itek replied doggedly, "because you'll smuggle them aboard."

"I'll what?"

Itek frowned. Lando's attitude was making him angry. "You'll smuggle them on board. That's what you *do*, isn't it? Smuggle things from one place to another? Well, here's a chance to show off."

"You're crazy, you know that?" Lando demanded. "Totally out of your mind. I don't do that anymore, but if I did it would take weeks of planning, and you're starting to piss me off!"

"Oh, I am, am I?" Itek demanded, his voice dangerously soft. "Well, consider this, *Citizen* Lando, either keep the deal you made, or get ready to spend the rest of your life on a prison planet!

"Now listen carefully. You're going to take the explosives I give you, plus some weapons, and place them in that trick suitcase you brought aboard. You know, the one with the secret compartment and the fancy electronics.

"Yes, I searched your belongings, just as I would *anyone* accused of murder. Then you're going to get that bag through Devo's security check or die trying. Do you read me, mister?"

There was a long silence as the two men stared each other down. Part of Lando wanted to say, "To hell with it, do your worst," but there was another part as well, the part that said, "He's right, you know, it *could* work, and if it does you keep the gold." The second part won.

"I read you, Lieutenant," Lando said finally, "and we'll do it *your* way, but on one condition. Once we get aboard *I* call the shots. Take it or leave it."

Itek smiled. "I'll take it. Now, let's cut the crap, and spend the rest of our time getting ready."

About four hours later the scout snuggled up against the space station's number one lock. The trip only took twenty minutes or so, but for security reasons only one ship was allowed to dock with Devo's Disk at any one time, so there was a long wait while other vessels loaded and unloaded passengers and cargo.

Lando and Itek were crammed into the ship's tiny lock. Both wore light-duty space suits with semiflex helmets pushed back over their shoulders. A bit cautious, but not unheard of when venturing onto a strange habitat, and not something to alarm Devo's security people.

As they waited for Martinez to complete the docking maneuver, Lando turned to Itek. "There's still something you haven't told me."

Itek grinned innocently. "Really? What's that?"

"Who we're after. It might help if I knew their names."

"Good point," Itek agreed mockingly. "Well, the answer is that we're after a man named Daniel Devo, and his wife Suzanne. They're the ones who murdered Nugleo."

Lando narrowed his eyes. "I hope that's your idea of a joke, Itek, because if it isn't, we're dead men."

"Don't be so pessimistic," Itek replied calmly. "He's just a man like you and me. Besides, we'll have the advantage of surprise. This is his home, his castle, the last place where anyone would attack him."

Lando felt pinpricks of sweat pop out all over his body. Anger rose and threatened to overwhelm him. Lando fought to keep his voice steady. "Why didn't you tell me?"

"Would you have come?"

"No."

"I rest my case."

Contact was made, air pressures were equalized, and Martinez came over the intercom. "Have fun, gentlemen. Let me know when to pick you up."

Lando swore softly and stepped onto Devo's Disk. The lock was huge, large enough to handle fifty people at once, or a load of containerized cargo. As a little boy he'd wondered why. His father had forced him to reason it out, to think about the colonists, and the kinds of emergencies they might face.

What if they need to get in or out in a hurry? What if the other even larger lock was damaged? What if they had to decontaminate everything that entered or left the ship?

Lando smiled. Come to think of it his father had been good at that, good at answering a question with a question, good at forcing him to think. What should he be thinking now?

Lando swallowed the lump in his throat as he stepped out of the lock and the hatch closed behind them. Martinez was gone by now, making room for another ship at the lock, and waiting for their signal. A signal that wouldn't come if they were dead. Lando pushed the thought down and back.

The reception area was even larger than the lock and full of people. All kinds of people. Glancing around, Lando saw leather-clad pirates, syntho-suited merchants, utilitarian rim worlders, and a dozen more. Some were preparing to leave and others were in the final stages of arrival.

A woman in gray body armor used a nerve lash to point out the green line painted on the deck. She had stringy blond hair and a bored expression.

"Welcome aboard. Follow the green line to the scanners please."

With Itek at his heels Lando followed the line through the crowd and arrived in front of the checkpoint just as a couple of middle-aged women passed through it. They looked cool and relaxed, but why not? They weren't toting a suitcase full of weapons and explosives. As the women disappeared through a blast-proof door Lando wished that he were going with them.

Glancing around, Lando saw lots of security scanners, four gray-clad security guards, and enough remote-controlled weapons to stop anything short of a marine assault team.

A man stepped forward. He had a hard face, muscular arms, and the word "SECURITY" stenciled across the front of his sculpted body armor. His voice had a singsong quality.

"This is Devo's Disk. We have rules. Break the rules and you will die. Rule one. All visitors must be unarmed. That includes projectile weapons, energy weapons, fixed blades, power blades, thrown weapons, explosives, nerve gas, poisons, toxins, lethal life forms, and any other device or organism that can be used to injure or kill sentient beings. If you have such weapons, surrender them now. You can collect them when you leave."

Lando was conscious of the bag. It felt heavier now, as if the explosives and the weapons had somehow doubled in weight, and were dragging the little suitcase toward the deck.

Receiving no reply the man continued. "Rule two. In order to come aboard Devo's Disk you must be known or sponsored by someone who is. Are you known?"

"I am," Lando responded, "and Citizen La Paz here has my sponsorship."

Though the naval officer hadn't said as much, Lando assumed he was a member of naval intelligence, raising the possibility that his name had found its way into Devo's data base. With that in mind they'd agreed to call him La Paz instead.

The guard nodded. "Place both feet on the yellow X."

As Lando stepped forward, the latticework of security scanners whined and shifted subtly.

"Stand still."

Lando did as he was told. An invisible scale weighed him, beams of light checked his height, ultrasonics probed the density of his body, an eye mapper scanned his retinas, while X rays slid through his suit and inventoried the contents of his suitcase. Or tried to, because the electronics hidden inside the bag took the X rays and did mysterious things with them.

This was it, possibly the most dangerous moment they'd face, and Lando fought to sublimate his fear. It was choking the breath from him, pushing his pulse upward, and causing his eyelids to blink. All things the machines could measure.

"There's only one way to beat your fear, son," his father had said, "and that's to accept it. Remember that it's there to help you, to protect you from danger, to keep you alive. So acknowledge your fear but get outside of it at the same time."

Lando wasn't sure if it was the advice, or the process of thinking about it, but suddenly he could breathe again.

The guard spoke again. "Thank you, Citizen Lando. You may step forward. You and your guest may proceed."

Lando nodded. The blast-proof hatch whirred open. Itek stepped through with Lando close behind. As the hatch slid closed the two men found themselves in a spotless corridor. Lando set a brisk pace. The sooner the whole thing was over the better.

The bulkheads were cream-colored and so heavily layered with paint that Lando could barely see the countless rivets that held the ship together. The deck was spotless and polished to a high gloss. A maze of pipes and electrical conduit ran overhead, each one carefully color-coded, and all bright with fresh paint.

"Amazing," Itek said as he looked around. "Absolutely amazing."

"Why's that?" Lando asked absently. Most of his attention was on the task ahead.

"It's so clean, like a battleship ready for inspection, or a first-class hospital."

Lando glanced his way, saw the other man was serious, and gave a derisive snort. "Oh, I get it. Criminals are filth, ergo, so are their quarters. You're the one who's 'amazing.' This isn't some frontier world bar, it's headquarters for an extremely successful business, and it's maintained accordingly."

"Oh, I see," Itek replied sarcastically. "A nice *clean* business built on drugs and murder."

Lando started to reply but thought better of it. No matter what he said Itek would find a way to twist it into something unpleasant.

Devo's Disk was laid out like a wheel. There were three main corridors. One followed the outer circumference of the hull, one circled the vessel halfway in, and one formed a perimeter around the command and control center located at the vessel's hub.

The outermost corridor was identified as "A," the middle corridor was labeled "B," and the innermost corridor was called "C."

The corridors were connected by spokelike passageways that were numbered "P-1" through "P-16" and radiated out from the command and control center to provide quick access to all sections of the ship. They were filled with people, coming, going, or just standing around. None showed any interest in Itek or Lando.

Itek started to say something, but Lando shook his head. "No you don't. My turn, remember?"

Lando led the other man inward, jogging left on corridor B, and checking to see if they had a tail. None was visible. Good. The last thing they needed was trouble with a security snoop or some bounty hunter.

Picking up passageway seven they followed it in toward the command and control center. That's where Devo and his wife should be, *would* be, if they were aboard, and Lando felt mixed emotions. On the one hand it would be a tremendous relief if the Devos were somewhere else, but on the other he'd be disappointed as well, having risked everything for nothing.

Suddenly the smell of food found Lando's nostrils and his stomach growled in response. A section of P-7 was given over to food and recreation vendors, all of whom paid a percentage of their profits to Devo. A wide variety of food, booze, and sex was available. Most of it was intended for humans, but some was geared for aliens, or those interested in a little cross-species experimentation. Like the rest of the ship P-7 was absolutely spotless.

Eventually the restaurants and bars gave way to a series of engineering spaces, followed by the hydroponics section, and a heavily secured data-processing facility. Corridor C was just ahead.

From exploring the ship as a child Lando knew there were four airtight doors that provided access to the command and control center, one off P-1, one off P-4, one off P-8, and one off P-12.

Of these P-1 was the most heavily used and the only door open to the public.

Lando took a right on corridor C and headed for the point where it would intersect with P-1.

Itek drew alongside. "Where are we . . ."

"Shut up and listen. In a few minutes we'll arrive at the command and control center. I'll ask the receptionist if the Devos are in. Assuming they are, we'll force our way into their private quarters, get them into their suits, and set the explosives. The ceiling of their cabin should correspond with the outside surface of the hull. After that we make a hole and hope for the best. Understand?"

Itek frowned. "Yes, but . . ."

"No buts," Lando snapped. "The sooner we move the better. There's the command and control center, so get ready."

The command and control center was clearly marked and softly lit. The general impression was of hushed efficiency with only the hum of office machines and the whisper of ventilation to mar the otherwise perfect silence.

Antique furniture squatted here and there, beautiful in its own right, but slightly out of phase with the painted metal behind it. The walls were decorated with an assortment of curiosities ranging from old flintlock pistols to alien hand tools.

The only person present was a balding middle-aged man. He sat behind a glass-topped desk empty of everything but a comset and a single sheet of paper.

He was dressed in an immaculate business suit with a Devo logo over the left breast pocket. Light glinted off an enormous gold pinkie ring as the man brought a hand up to straighten his old-fashioned glasses. "Yes?"

The word spoke volumes. It said, "This is the center of the known universe, all that happens here is under *my* control, and you would do well to keep that in mind."

Lando produced his brightest smile and placed his suitcase in the middle of the man's desk. "Hello there. Are the Devos in?"

The man was both startled and taken aback. He moved back and away from the sudden invasion of his personal space. "What? Why yes . . . I mean no . . . not unless you have an appointment."

"No problem then," Lando said, unzipping the bag, " 'cause we've got an appointment. As a matter of fact . . . here's our invitation."

So saying Lando withdrew a hand blaster and aimed it at the man's head. As he did so the smuggler was careful to keep his body between the weapon and the doorway behind him.

"Close the door please, and as you do so, make damn sure you hit the right button. If a squad of security people show up you'll be the first to die."

The man's jaw worked soundlessly as he stared into the blaster's bore and pressed a button at the same time.

Lando heard the double doors whir closed behind him and gave a sigh of relief. So far so good. No one would interrupt them at least.

"Now, send a little message to security. Tell them why you closed the doors, and whatever story you use, it'd better be good."

The man gave a jerky nod and swallowed. He touched the lower right-hand corner of his desk. A backlit keyboard appeared in the glass. As he typed, the words appeared on the upper portion of the desk. Lando read them upside down as Itek reached inside the bag for a blaster.

"Essex to security. Closed for two hours. D."

Itek used his blaster to point at the words. "What the hell does that mean?"

"Just what it says," Essex replied icily. "I shut down at Mr. Devo's request from time to time. No other reason is required." Essex was starting to recover now that the original shock was over.

"Fine," Lando replied. "Now back away from the desk. Good . . . Now I want you to . . ."

Lando never finished his sentence, because at that moment an entire section of bulkhead slid open, and Daniel Devo stepped through.

He was a big man with a mane of white hair, bushy eyebrows to match, and a ruddy complexion. He wore gray overalls with his own logo on the pocket, a utility belt, and a pair of knee-high black boots. Devo held a sheaf of printouts in his right hand.

"Essex . . . where are the . . ." He stopped suddenly at the sight of two men with blasters. "What the hell?"

" 'What the hell' indeed," Itek said, easing his way around Devo. "Where's your wife?"

Devo frowned, his bushy white brows coming together in a solid line. "I'll be damned if I'll tell you. This is hopeless you know. There are only two ways off this ship and both are guarded."

A woman appeared in the doorway. She was a good twenty years younger than Devo and quite beautiful. She had long black hair, even features, and a well-sculpted body.

"Dan? What's going on? I . . ."

"Ah," Itek said, checking to be sure Lando had both men covered before shifting his aim to the woman. "Suzanne Devo I presume. And just in time for the party. Stand over there next to your husband."

Lando frowned. Something was wrong. What was Itek doing? Why bring her into the reception area when he should do just the opposite? Surely the Devos' space suits were located in their living quarters.

"Now," Itek said, "you're probably wondering what this is all about. The answer's simple. I'm an officer in the Imperial navy. A few weeks ago you killed an Imperial Courier, and now you must pay. Any questions?"

Devo looked from Itek to Lando and back, as if checking their sanity. "Pay? It's money you want? Why didn't you say so? I'm sure we can . . ."

There was a burp of blue light as Itek fired. As Suzanne Devo fell she revealed a scorch mark on the wall behind her.

Lando spun toward the right. "Itek . . . what the hell are you . . ."

But it was too late. Devo was already in motion. The flint-lock pistol came off the wall brackets with ease and made a loud bang as it went off. The lead sphere hit Itek right between the eyes and went out through the back of his head.

Lando fired more on instinct than thought, his first bolt catching Devo in the stomach, the second hitting the top of his head as he fell. There was an audible thump as Devo hit the floor and perfect silence after that.

Essex and Lando looked at each other, both too shocked to move, both struggling to take it in. Itek has murdered Suzanne Devo in cold blood, not only that, he'd planned it all along. All the talk about taking them back had been little more than a ruse designed to gain Lando's cooperation.

Essex moved slightly and Lando's blaster moved with him. "Hold it right there."

Essex obeyed.

"Sit on your hands."

Essex stood, slid his hands under his ample rear end, and sat down again. Sweat covered the whiteness of his forehead and his lower lip trembled. Lando was a ruthless killer as far as Essex was concerned.

"Don't move."

Removing a length of monofilament line from his suitcase Lando tied Essex to his chair. With any luck at all the other man would be immobilized long enough for Lando's escape.

After taking one last look around, Lando grabbed his suitcase, stepped into Devo's private quarters, and hit a wall switch. The door slid closed behind him with a soft thud.

The Devos' quarters seemed small but were large by shipboard standards. Lando saw thick carpeting, a profusion of antiques, and the same soft lighting as the reception area. Wait a minute, what was that?

Moving left Lando saw a raised area, a sleeping loft, and hurried that way. The loft would save him the time involved in moving furniture around so he could reach the overhead.

Bounding up a short flight of steps Lando looked upward and laughed. There mounted flush with the overhead was a metal frame and hatch. A lock! An emergency escape lock. Of course! The Devos' back door. Would the lock alert security if he used it? Did it matter? After all, it should attract less attention than blowing a hole in the hull, and even if it didn't, the fact that the lock belonged to Devo might slow them down.

Lando climbed up onto the Devos' bed. From there it was easy to push the red button.

The lock opened with a hiss of escaping air. A motor whined and a ladder slid down. Lando reached back to pull his helmet on. When the helmet was in place Lando double-checked his seals, pressurized the suit, and climbed the ladder.

After that it was a simple matter of pushing another red button, waiting for the ladder to retract, and sealing the hatch. Three minutes later the lock was depressurized and open to space.

Lando felt a momentary lightness as he stepped out onto the surface of the ship's hull and left artificial gravity behind. Then the electromagnets in his boots kicked in and the feeling passed.

Reaching down Lando activated the small transmitter attached to his utility belt and removed two laser flares. He flicked them on and they strobed in unison. The response was almost instantaneous.

Martinez had already brought the scout in so close that Devos' security people were chewing her out when the unbroken tone came across her headset.

Cutting them off in midsentence Martinez added power and brought the scout in. It was something to see. Lando watched in admiration as Martinez came in only inches off the larger vessel's hull, paused while he climbed aboard, and accelerated away.

A few minutes later he was out of the space suit and strapped in beside her. "Any pursuit?"

Martinez kept her eyes on the instruments. "Yeah, but it's too little, too late. We go hyper thirty-three seconds from now."

"How 'bout the rail gun?"

Martinez smiled thinly. "They've been shooting at us for two minutes now and haven't hit us yet. Not all antiques work as well as that flintlock pistol did."

Lando started to say something but the NAVCOMP picked that moment to enter hyperspace. He felt the usual nausea and swallowed hard. With no nav beacon for a reference point random hyperspace jumps could be extremely dangerous. It was soon apparent however that Itek had anticipated this very situation and calculated the coordinates ahead of time. Another reason he and Martinez were so blasé about the rail gun.

Lando turned to Martinez and this time she met his gaze. "How did you know about the flintlock?"

She shrugged. "I watched the whole thing live."

"You what?"

"I watched the whole thing live. There was a vid pickup and thin beam transmitter built into both of your suits. You didn't think we'd send Itek in there without keeping some sort of record did you?"

She shook her head sadly. "Itek must have felt real stupid just before he died, a flintlock for God's sake, but them's the breaks. You got it done and Essex will spread the news: 'Couriers are untouchable.' Case closed."

"Just like that?"

Martinez gave a snort of derision. "Sure, 'just like that.' What? You want me to cry 'cause Itek was an overconfident jerk? Amateurs. Get some rest, Lando. I'll have you home in no time."

10

Lando was sipping his second cup of coffee when Cy and Melissa burst into *Junk*'s galley.

It had been a week since his return and things were back to normal. In this case "normal" meant Cap was "sick" a good deal of the time causing Lando to shoulder most of the work, but what else was new? At least Cap had continued the cleanup effort during Lando's absence and met the minimum terms of their contract. There was still a week or two of work left to be done but the end was in sight.

Lando had considered leaving, taking his share of the gold, and buying a passage out, but what good would that do? He'd still be persona non grata with the underworld and have a price on his head everywhere else.

So, until Lando could figure a way out of his double bind, *Junk* was a place to be. More than that, a place where he was accepted, and no different from all the rest. Lando raised his coffee mug in a mock salute.

"Greetings, O princess of space. Salutations, O silver one."

Melissa curtsied in reply, while Cy rolled forward, then backward, suggesting a bow. Having done so, both were silent.

There was something about them however, something about the repressed excitement in Melissa's eyes and the way Cy bobbed up and down that suggested an agenda of some sort.

Lando raised an eyebrow. "Well?"

Cy turned a vid pickup in Melissa's direction and she looked back. It was Cy who spoke. "Well, I've been overhauling the drives, and we've got a problem."

Lando took another sip of coffee. "I'm listening."

"It's the control module for the number two power accumulator," Melissa put in eagerly. "It was nearly worn out so Cy installed our backup."

"And that means we need a *new* backup," Cy continued. "So we wondered if you would . . ."

"Take the two of you dirtside," Lando finished dryly. "And once there you could have a little fun. What's Cap say?"

"Well, that's the problem," Melissa said innocently, "he's sick, and that means you're in charge."

Although Cap had never formally designated Lando as second in command, it was understood and accepted by all concerned.

Lando smiled at the obvious attempt to manipulate him. Both knew full well that Cap would say no.

Ever since the brawl back on Dista, and his own trip to the surface of Pylax, Sorenson had shown a marked aversion to going dirtside. The reason was fairly obvious. Jord Willer was out to get him and his crew. By maintaining a low profile Cap hoped to avoid trouble. Not only that, but Cap was still fixated on the *Star Of Empire,* and had little interest in anything else. Anything outside of a bottle that is.

Lando put the mug down. What the hell, staying cooped up on a spaceship was no life for a little girl, or a cyborg either for that matter. A trip dirtside would do them all a lot of good. The odds against running into Willer were astronomically large. He smiled.

"The shuttle for Pylax leaves in thirty minutes. There's some civilized people down there . . . so dress accordingly."

About four hours later they stepped out of the tender, hired an auto cab, and departed in style. It took only a few minutes to cross the scorched duracrete, buy the control module from one of the many suppliers that lined the edge of the spaceport, and head downtown.

Melissa chattered like a magpie as they rolled through Blast Town, while Cy zipped from one side of the cab to the other, and Lando looked out the window.

There were people everywhere, walking, talking, doing things. And because this was Blast Town some were certain to be bounty hunters. Were they looking for him? Sorting through memprinted faces in search of his? Lando forced the thought out of his mind. To hell with them. He deserved some time off and by God he'd have it.

The auto cab passed through the downtown area and headed for the suburbs. They'd agreed that each person could choose one activity and this was Cy's. Though trapped aboard ship for the past few weeks, the cyborg had access to all the planet's vid channels, and that's how he'd heard about bacca racing.

Baccas were little eight-legged weasellike animals that could run up to thirty or forty miles an hour. Racing them, and betting on those races, was extremely popular on Pylax and Cy was eager to see the real thing.

The cab slid into a tube way where it surrendered control to the city's transportation computer. Interior lights came on as the cab picked up speed and headed underground.

Outside the windows dark duracrete rolled by, occasionally relieved by the sight of vehicles headed in the opposite direction, and platforms full of waiting passengers.

Melissa passed the time by making faces in the glass. Seeing this Cy got into the act too. First he floated beside Melissa, so she had two heads instead of one, then he hid behind her and made a vid pickup grow out of her ear.

Outside the cab there were occasional flashes of sunlight as the cab shuttled up and down between surface and subsurface tubes.

Then, just when Lando was wondering if the trip would ever end, they rolled out of a hillside and onto a regular road. The cab coasted downhill toward a huge recreational complex.

The building had a dome-shaped roof and, thanks to a mineral mixed into the duracrete, glittered like gold. Huge parking lots surrounded the facility and were packed to overflowing with brightly colored ground cars.

Meanwhile, Cy was bobbing up and down with excitement and counting out the money he'd produced from a hidden compartment. Seeing this, Lando was reminded of how Cy had gambled away his body, and wondered if coming here was such a good idea after all.

But good idea or not Cy was clearly determined to go inside. So, rather than challenge him, Lando resolved to give it some time and ease the cyborg out of the complex as quickly as possible.

The cab pulled up at the main entrance, agreed to debit Cap's bank account, and whirred off with a new fare.

Cy generated a few stares as they joined the throng that was crowding its way into the dome, but so did the scattering of other cyborgs, and nobody looked for very long. Lando was glad figuring that people who stared at Cy wouldn't notice him.

The inside of the building was a large open space. Various kinds of vendors lined the outside walls. The crowd seemed to have divided itself into subgroups and headed toward various parts of the huge floor. Once there they seemed to mill around.

Lando couldn't see the attraction at first, but then he caught a glimpse of a boxlike structure at the center of each group, and realized it was a computer terminal.

"That's how you place your bets," Cy explained eagerly, "the terminals will accept cash or credit. You can bet on a particular animal to win, place, or draw."

"That's nice," Lando said, looking around. "But where are they? The animals I mean? And how can they race with all the people in here?"

All of a sudden the lights dimmed, there was a flurry of trumpets, and a melodic voice flooded the PA system. "Fellow sentients! Welcome to the Pylax Pavilion! Are you ready for a bounty of bodacious baccas? Let me hear you say 'Hell yes!' "

"Hell yes!" the crowd roared back, and Lando realized that a small army of booze and drug vendors had started to make their rounds. With each passing moment the pavilion seemed less and less appropriate for little girls.

"That's the announcer Les Lexus," Cy yelled over the noise. "Isn't he a riot?"

"Yeah, a real riot," Lando agreed dryly. "Do you think this is a good place for Melissa?"

Cy spun back and forth as if seeing the pavilion in a new way. "Well, now that you mention it I'm . . ."

There was another blare of trumpets. Four holo projections, one for every point on the compass, snapped into being, each one filled with statistics on that day's races. Then the ceiling became a maze of pulsating red, blue, yellow, and green neon, while the floor turned suddenly transparent. "Lando, look!"

Lando followed Melissa's finger down toward the floor. What he saw was a softly lit transparent tube. A brown streak raced through it and Lando realized that he'd just seen a bacca.

It was running through a complex system of tunnels under the pavilion's floor. Looking closer he saw there were actually two tracks, the one that was lit, and another more complicated version right next to it.

A cheer went up. "Warm-ups are under way . . . it's time to place your bets, my fellow sapients . . . time to win, lose, or draw!"

Lando turned to say something to Cy but he was gone. Standing on tiptoe, Lando could just make him out, placing his bet at a terminal, then speeding back.

"Just one race," Cy said excitedly, braking himself with a jet of compressed air, "then we'll leave. One race won't corrupt you will it, Mel?"

"Of course not!" Melissa replied indignantly. "Besides, I want to see what happens. How does it work, Cy?"

"Well," Cy replied, taking on the air of a lecturing professor, "first the tunnels are misted with rasa scent, those are the little animals that baccas like to hunt, and then four of them are released all at once.

"That's no problem at first, because the tunnel's real wide, but then it narrows down and that forces 'em to go through one at a time."

"And what happens then?" Lando asked, already having a pretty good idea.

"Well," Cy said cautiously, sensing the trap that had just been laid for him, "they tussle a bit. You know, fight to see who goes first."

"But that's mean!" Melissa said unhappily. "You're making them fight!"

"Maybe a little," Cy admitted, "but they rarely get hurt. Then the tunnel widens out a bit, and two baccas can run neck and neck till they hit the maze."

"The maze?" Melissa asked suspiciously. "What happens there?"

"Here, I'll show you." Cy zipped over toward a cluster of people and waited for Lando and Melissa to arrive. Looking down they saw that what had been a single tunnel was now a maze of tubing, complete with twists, turns, false entrances, and dead ends.

"There's only one way through," Cy said, "and they've got to find it. Once they do there's an underwater swim, an obstacle course, and a long straightaway to the finish line. The first one across wins."

Melissa crossed her arms and tapped a small foot. Then she frowned and gave Cy a dirty look. "I think it's silly and mean. I hope you lose all your money."

But this comment was lost on Cy as a bell clanged, a cheer went up, and the announcer yelled, "They're off!"

Something moved up above. Lando looked up to find that the pulsating neon had resolved itself into a huge diagram. Since spectators could see little more than the section of tunnel where they happened to be standing, the diagram provided the "big" picture, and served as a universal reference point.

Meanwhile, a small army of antigrav-equipped robo-cams had appeared all over the inside of the pavilion and were feeding images to the holos above. The pictures were the same ones seen all over the planet.

Choosing the diagram over actual video Lando watched as four animated baccas were released from a stylized starting gate. At first they were side by side, racing down a short straightaway, heading for the point where the tunnel narrowed.

Then, as the passageway began to close in, the cartoon baccas began to nip each other trying to gain an advantage. It was immediately clear that numbers one and four were getting the best of it, but just when their supremacy seemed assured, the tunnel ballooned out, then narrowed into a tiny corridor.

The crowd cheered as the electronic baccas tore into each other, biting off chunks of neon-colored flesh in their eagerness to pursue the maddening scent, each determined to be first through the hole.

Looking down, Lando saw that Melissa was undisturbed. Like him she was watching the computerized animation and the cartoonlike images held no reality for her.

Half the crowd cheered and the other half groaned as number three wriggled through the passageway first. Numbers one, four, and two were close on its heels.

Cy yelled, "Here they come!"

Lando looked up and saw the cyborg was right. The crowd was coming toward them with two robo-cams leading the way. He grabbed Melissa's shoulder just as the mob surged around them.

"Look!" Melissa said and pointed toward the floor.

Lando looked just in time to see four furry little animals enter the transparent maze. An extremely small robo-cam followed along behind them.

Each bacca wore a harness with a number on it. They had small weasellike faces, no external ears, and three eyes. One eye was located up front toward the center of the bacca's head, with the other two on either side, providing lateral vision.

Lando noticed that their front legs were shorter, ended in prehensile paws, and weren't used for running. Would a few million years of additional evolution turn their front legs into arms and their paws into hands? There was no way to tell.

Number three was bleeding profusely from a deep bite. Melissa bit a knuckle and reached for Lando's hand.

Now Lando found that he could see individual differences between the animals.

Number one darted here and there, exploring each and every possible route, eliminating them one by one.

Two was different, more tentative somehow, sniffing here and there but refusing to make a commitment.

Three split its time between licking its wound and exploring, while four sat back and took it all in. Was it thinking? Or just so confused it didn't know what to do?

The question was answered a few seconds later when number four took off down a tube, took two turns to the right, and cleared the maze.

A few seconds later numbers one, two, and three confirmed what Lando was beginning to suspect, that baccas are smarter than they look, and followed four's lead. As usual the small robo-cam tagged along behind them.

As the animals headed toward the underwater swim, most of the crowd followed, pulling Cy along. A few moments later Lando and Melissa had the surface of the maze all to themselves.

"Well," Lando said, "what do you think?"

"I think it's mean," Melissa answered without hesitation. "I felt sorry for number three. Will he be okay?"

"I'm sure he will," Lando answered reassuringly. "How 'bout some ice cream while we wait?"

"Yes please!" Melissa said, jumping up and down with excitement. Seconds later she had him by the hand and was towing him toward the nearest refreshment counter.

Looking back over his shoulder, Lando saw Cy hovering over the thickest part of the crowd and decided the cyborg would have little trouble finding them. Life in a silver sphere might have its problems but it had some advantages too.

It was a full fifteen minutes later before the baccas had found the way over, through, and around all the obstacles, and made the final dash for the finish line. Number two was first, with four second, three third, and one last. The winners roared with approval, while the losers threw their tickets toward the floor in disgust and ordered some more solace from one of the many vendors.

Cy appeared out of nowhere, shouting, "I won! I won!" before speeding off toward a nearby pay-out window. Lando and Melissa traded amused grins as they ambled along behind. They were about fifty feet from the window when all hell broke loose.

Someone shouted, "Grab that cyborg!" and the crowd swirled as a dozen people tried to obey.

Lando looked up just in time to see a man throw his cape over Cy and attempt to bundle him up. Two men and a woman stepped in to assist while Melissa ran straight at them shouting, "Let him go! He hasn't done anything to you! Let him go!"

Lando swore a blue streak as he followed, cursing Cy, cursing himself, and cursing his rotten luck. The four strangers had Cy almost under control by the time he arrived, but a flying body block and a bite or two from Melissa turned the tide.

Breaking out from under the cape, Cy squirted himself upward, and yelled, "Follow me!" So saying he headed for the nearest exit.

Breaking free of the hands that reached out to grab him, Lando grabbed Melissa's arm and followed the fleeing cyborg. He didn't get far. The stunner hit him right square between the shoulder blades.

Lando dropped like a rock. He could see and hear but that was all. All of his muscles were locked into spasm. People yelled, robo-cams swarmed around him like flies on a corpse, and rough hands picked him up off the floor. Since Lando was facedown he saw nothing but floor.

Lando heard a man say, "Yeah, the gambler's guild wants

the borg for unpaid debts, and this guy tried to help him escape. The girl says her father's a Captain somebody or other. Book 'em and let the judge sort it out."

Lando gave a silent groan. Surely things couldn't get any worse than this?

But had Lando seen the bounty hunter with the green eyes and the flaming red hair he would've known the answer. Things *could* get worse. Much, much worse.

11

Like most jails this one was less than pleasant. Though the structure itself was reasonably modern, the inmates were the same scum who filled prisons everywhere, and something less than pleasant.

Lando had been in four fights during the last twelve hours. Two involved protecting Cy from other prisoners, one centered around keeping his boots, and the last centered around his portion of slop the guards referred to as "dinner."

Lando won all four, but with a constant flow of prisoners in and out of the holding pen, he'd soon be forced to prove himself again.

The pen was roughly seventy-five feet long and about fifteen feet wide. At the moment a hundred twenty-three men shared this relatively small space and it was an extremely tight fit.

Some lounged on the metal benches that lined two of the four walls, a few lay unconscious on the floor, and the rest stood around talking. Their conversation centered around sex and money mostly, with overtones of "What're you in for?" And "When you gettin' out?"

For the most part they were all the same, drunks, addicts, petty thieves, and pimps. Rumor had it there was another nicer jail for important criminals like homicidal maniacs.

The front of the holding cell featured floor-to-ceiling bars. Cy wanted to cut them using the torch concealed inside his metal torso, but Lando forbid him to do so, pointing out that they were in enough trouble without engineering a mass escape.

So the two of them were snuggled into a much contested corner waiting for something to happen. Something that was way overdue. By now Cap should have sobered up, come dirtside, and bailed them out.

And how about Melissa? Shortly after the arrest the police had taken her somewhere else. Somewhere nicer than where *he* was Lando hoped. But where was that? Had Sorenson come for Melissa and left the rest of his crew behind? Given the mess they were in Cap might consider such an action completely justified. There was no way to know.

There was a stir toward the front of the cell. "Pik Lando! Pik Lando, front and center!" The voice belonged to a guard.

Lando looked at Cy. The cyborg activated his antigrav unit and squirted himself toward the ceiling. He'd be out of reach up there, and as luck would have it, the bullies who'd bothered him earlier were out on bail.

Seeing Lando's concern Cy did his best to sound unconcerned. "Don't worry, Pik, I'm good for a few hours yet, I'll see you later."

Lando nodded. He had very little choice. Maybe they'd call Cy's name next. A fight started over the rights to his corner as Lando made his way toward the front of the cell.

The guard was small as guards go, with a small man's chip on his shoulder, and a slug gun to back it up. He had a blue plastic bag in his left hand. There was some sort of official seal stamped on the front of it.

"Are you Pik Lando?"

Lando nodded.

"Stand in the red circle."

Lando stood in the red circle and waited for the door to slide open.

"Step outside."

Lando did as he was told and heard the door slide closed behind him.

"Follow the red line. One step off it and I'll blow your brains our through your smile."

Lando followed the solid red line. It led down the corridor, through a heavily secured blast-proof door, and into a brightly lit interrogation chamber.

The room was white except for some suspicious-looking stains on the walls and floor. There were a couple of sturdy-looking wooden chairs and a table with a plastic top. A woman with bright red hair, green eyes, and a nice figure perched on one corner.

Lando took her for a cop at first, then realized his mistake and felt something heavy hit his stomach. A bounty hunter! It was written all over her. The casual stance, the cross-draw holster, the amused expression as he figured it out. What the hell was going on?

The guard smiled. The bounty hunter was only slightly taller than he and nice to look at. "Is this the one?"

"That's him," Della Dee agreed, "one Pik Lando, wanted for murder and interplanetary flight to avoid prosecution. Bounty number WMH 56843-F. Here's my license."

Dee stood up to hand the guard a ragged piece of plastic.

The guard gave the license a cursory glance and handed it back. "Did you plead him guilty and pay his fine?"

"Signed, sealed, and delivered. Here's the receipt."

The guard waved it away. "You headin' off-planet? I know a place that sells a great steak . . . real stuff . . . Terran stock."

Dee produced a thousand-megawatt smile and a well-worn pair of handcuffs. "Sounds wonderful! I haven't had a good steak in a zillion rotations. Gotta take a rain check though . . . my ship lifts at 0200 hours."

The guard was obviously disappointed. "Darn, that's too bad. Need any help with those cuffs?"

"Don't think so," Dee replied, pulling Lando's arms behind his back and closing the cuffs with a practiced hand. "You just show us the door and we'll be on our way."

"You got it," the guard replied. He handed her the blue bag. "Don't forget this. It's his personal effects. Money, a handgun, and some sort of wrist-mounted missile launcher."

"What?" Dee asked as she accepted the bag. "No energy cannon?"

The guard laughed and Dee smiled in return. In spite of her flip comment however, Dee remembered Dista, and Lando lying on the floor with the cyborg towering over him. Maybe he had good reasons for toting an arsenal. An arsenal he could've used inside the pavilion but hadn't.

The guard opened the door and Dee nodded at Lando. He

stepped through the door and into the hall. He was careful to stay relaxed, to give her the impression that he'd given up. His chance would come, but not here and not now.

The guard said good-bye, and bit by bit they made their way through a succession of security checkpoints and into the cool night air.

Each lamppost cast a pool of greenish-blue light, and the pools marched off into the distance, until they were little more than dots.

A steady stream of cops and robbers came and went around them as Dee directed Lando to a parked ground car. She opened the back door and gestured for him to get inside. He didn't move.

Dee pulled her slug gun and held it to Lando's head. "Get in the car or I'll blow your head off and send your retinas in for identification."

Lando forced himself to ignore the gun. "I believe you, but before we get in that car, I want to know *who* you are and *where* we're going."

Dee nodded, but the gun stayed where it was. "Fair enough. My name's Della Dee. You're wanted on Ithro so that's where we're going."

"I suppose the fact that I'm innocent doesn't matter."

"That's what they all say. Anything else?"

Lando raised an eyebrow. "Can you be bought?"

"Sure. Your bounty's two hundred and fifty thousand. Spot me that, plus another ten, and we'll have a drink."

Lando thought about it. Even with the gold he couldn't raise that much. He smiled. "Sorry, I'm two hundred short. Can we have the drink anyway?"

"Nope. Get in the car."

Lando obeyed and heard Dee lock the door behind him. The ground car was an upscale luxury job with a roomy interior.

Dee got in on the driver's side, dropped the blue bag onto the seat beside her, and started the engine.

"Nice car."

"Glad you like it," Dee replied cheerfully. "Only the best for you."

"Rental job, huh?"

"Yup."

"Kind of expensive isn't it?"

"I can afford it thanks to you," Dee replied as she pulled into traffic. "Besides, in my kind of business it pays to drive something heavy and fast."

"Yeah," Lando replied. "I suppose it does."

Both were silent for a while as Dee wove in and out of light traffic. They had just passed through the business district and entered Blast Town when Dee broke the silence.

"Do the people behind us belong to you?"

With some difficulty Lando managed to swivel around and look out the back window. There was a large hover truck right behind them. Dee changed lanes and the truck followed.

"I don't think so," Lando replied. "My people would follow in a taxi or something like that."

"I was afraid of that," Dee said grimly. "How 'bout that chrome-plated cyborg you waxed on Dista? Is there any chance he's after you?"

Lando thought about Jord Willer. "Yeah, he's a distinct possibility, although I can't see how he'd find me here."

"You've got to be kidding," Dee replied as she hit the gas and screeched around a corner. "The pavilion thing was all over the evening news. You were bound to make bail. They waited for you to come out."

Lando fell sideways. "Wait a minute, how come you know about Jord Willer?"

"Is that his name?" Dee asked, racing up an alley. "I was there when you shot him in the knees. Nice piece of work but stupid, Why so fancy? Why not grease him and be done with it?"

"Because I don't like killing people," Lando replied, bracing himself with his feet as white light filled the inside of the car and the truck rammed them from behind. "They're getting kind of close, aren't they?"

"Typical backseat driver," Dee replied evenly. "Uh-oh."

Lando looked up just in time to see another set of headlights coming straight at them. There was no place to go. Dee stood on the brakes and pulled her gun at the same time. "Keep your head down, Lando. It's worth a lot of money."

Dee opened her door and rolled out onto the pavement. A gun went off and the windshield shattered. There were two loud explosions as Dee returned fire followed by the stutter of an automatic weapon. Bullets stitched a line of holes along the car's roof line.

Meanwhile Lando struggled to move his handcuffed hands from back to front. The hardest part was passing them under his rear end. After that it was relatively easy, passing them along his thighs, and out from under his feet.

Dee fired three rounds from just outside the door. A man screamed. The car rocked as something made a deep booming sound and heavy projectiles hit the engine compartment. There was a popping sound and flames licked out from under the hood.

Lando dived over the seat and scrabbled for the blue bag. Finding it he swore when it refused to open. The cuffs made it even harder. Damn! Damn! Damn!

Then it was open and his fingers were closing around familiar grips. The mini-launcher would have been nice but there was no time to fool around with it. Opening the driver's side door he rolled out onto hard duracrete.

Dee was there, crouched by the rear tire, firing over the trunk. Someone opened up with a blaster. Dee ducked as the energy weapon cooked the paint off the car's roof and trunk. Seeing Lando she brought her pistol up, then let it drop.

"What the hell are you doing here? Thought I told you to keep your head down."

"I'd like to keep it period," Lando answered, offering the bounty hunter his manacled wrists. "How many and where?"

"About nine to begin with," Dee replied. She produced an electronic key and touched it to the cuffs. "I make it six now, two up front, and four behind."

The cuffs clattered as they hit the ground.

Lando nodded and rubbed his wrists. "Let's break out through the weak side."

Dee ejected a half-empty magazine and slapped a fresh one into the butt of her gun. "Sounds good to me. By the way . . ."

"Yeah?"

"When this is over I still plan to take you in."

Dee was up and running before Lando could reply. A gun flashed up ahead. Dee fired and heard a scream.

Something whipped by Lando's head followed by a sharp cracking sound. He turned, saw someone silhouetted against a distant streetlight, and fired. The figure jerked and fell.

There was a deep booming sound from Lando's left. He turned just in time to see Dee fall and Jord Willer step out of the shadows. Light rippled over the surface of the cyborg's chromed body. Willer held an automatic shotgun cradled in his arms. He was in the process of bringing it up when a cone of light pinned him to the ground.

The voice came from somewhere above. "You there! This is the police! Drop your weapons! I repeat, this is the . . ."

Someone fired and the spotlight snapped out. Lando rushed forward but the cyborg faded into the night. He turned to Dee. She lay in a crumpled heap. There was blood all over the place. Lando felt for her pulse. It was surprisingly strong. Her body armor had absorbed most of the blast.

Lando scooped her up and started to run. Behind him the spotlight came on again as a police floater drifted groundward. Lando had no plan at first, just an overwhelming need to be somewhere else, away from the police and Willer's thugs.

The fact that he got away was more luck than skill. Knowing that he should avoid the main streets, Lando stuck to the maze of passageways that connected Blast Town's back doors, and headed vaguely south.

Bit by bit the adrenaline ebbed away, and as it did, Dee got heavier. Not only that but he encountered other people, the kind that cling to the underside of society's rock, and appear only at night.

Pushers, addicts, organ runners, hookers, and more appeared and disappeared as Lando worked his way through dimly lit passageways and corridors. Most gave a wide berth when they saw Dee's blood-soaked clothing and his slug gun. Not so the street urchin who tugged at his left sleeve.

"Hey, mister, you wanta sell her? I'll get you top dollar for her lungs and kidneys."

"Get lost, kid."

"Oh," the little boy said understandingly. "You want to use her first. No problem. I'll get you a doctor. A *real* one who went to college and everything."

Lando stopped and draped Dee over his left shoulder. "Close by?"

The boy nodded eagerly. "You bet! A block, maybe two. The doc'll fix her up and whamo, it's party time!"

"Come here."

The urchin approached warily. Lando's hand shot out, grabbed the boy by his filthy shirt, and jerked him in close. He had blue eyes, a pug nose, and bad breath. "If you're lying I'll kill you."

"Who me?" the boy said innocently. "Never! I'll take you to the doc, no problem."

"You'd better," Lando said grimly, and released the boy's shirt.

Dee got even heavier as Lando followed the urchin through various twists and turns. By now her blood had soaked through his shirt.

A door opened up ahead, a rectangle of light hit the far side of the passageway, and the boy gestured Lando inside. "This is the place, mister. You take her inside, and the doc'll fix her good as new."

Lando looked through the open door, saw what looked like a reasonably clean reception area, and fumbled for some money. He didn't have any. It was in the blue bag.

Groping Dee's clothing, Lando found a sizable roll of currency in her right-hand pants pocket, and managed to pull it out. He peeled off some bills.

"Thanks, kid . . . you want some more of the same?"

The little boy nodded eagerly. "You bet! Whatcha want? Drugs? Booze? Some smokes?"

"None of the above. Just get me a taxi, and have it wait."

"You got it, mister," the boy said enthusiastically. "One taxi coming up!"

As the urchin disappeared into the darkness Lando stepped inside. The room was small but tidy, and smelled of disinfectants. There was a row of tubular chairs, a three-legged coffee table, and a curtained doorway.

"Can I help you?"

Lando looked around but couldn't locate the source.

"Down here," the voice said patiently, and Lando looked toward his feet. A small robot crouched there, looking more like a pile of oversize ball bearings than what it was.

"Yes," Lando replied. "We're here to see the doctor."

"Your timing is quite propitious," the robot observed. "The

doctor is in, and available for consultation. I note that you are carrying a young woman. Are you holding her for reproductive purposes or is she the patient?"

"She's the patient," Lando responded dryly, "and damned heavy. Where can I put her down?"

"Right through the curtained door," the robot said. "I will lead the way." So saying, four of the robot's round appendages began to spin, and carried it toward the door and under the curtain.

Lando followed and soon found himself in a small operating room. The reception robot had disappeared. A power-assisted table occupied the center of the space, overhung by a spotlessly clean light, and surrounded by glassed-in cabinets.

A woman stood in front of a set labeled "Closures" and was rummaging around inside. Hearing Lando enter she spoke without turning around.

"Put the patient on the table please."

Lando did as he was told. His heart leapt into his throat. Here, under good light, Dee looked terrible. Her face, her neck, everything was covered with blood.

"Let's have a look."

Lando turned and found himself face-to-face with an android. She was beautiful. Long dark hair framed a perfect face and reached down to touch the top of her white lab coat.

But her beauty had the hard, stiff quality of a fashion mannequin. Not because science couldn't *do* better, but because they didn't *want* to. Otherwise robots might pass for people, and that could lead to all sorts of problems. Yes, there was no mistaking the stiff features, the shininess of her skin, or the subtle whir of servos when she moved.

"Don't be alarmed," the android said reassuringly. "Though not considered adequate for the more creative and innovative aspects of medicine, my skills are sufficient for the task at hand. Your companion will be fine."

So saying the robot moved in, ran gentle hands up and down Dee's body, and went to work.

For the next hour or so Lando watched as the android cleaned, stitched, and bandaged. Although Dee's body armor had absorbed the worst of the shotgun blast she had wounds in her neck, shoulders, and upper arms.

In addition to patching up the holes in Dee's body the doctor gave her a blood volume expander laced with vitamins.

At one point she came to, tried to sit up, and passed out when the doctor slapped an injector against her arm.

Finally it was over and the android went over to sterilize her hands in some boiling water. "Your friend will be fine. She needs plenty of rest and some antibiotics that I will provide before you leave. Do you have any money?"

Lando nodded.

"Good. You will pay me two hundred credits. My fee is twice what the same services would cost at a public hospital but privacy has a price."

Lando counted the money onto a countertop. "There you go. One question . . ."

"Who am I? And what am I doing here?" the android asked, drying her hands under a blower. "Would you answer those same questions?"

Lando smiled and shook his head.

"Then neither will I," the robot replied gently. But then, just as she passed him, the light hit her face just so and Lando saw the faint outlines of something on her forehead. Something that looked remarkably like a logo for a huge conglomerate called Intersystems Incorporated. A logo that had been chemically erased.

A runaway robot! Lando had heard of such creatures but never met one. Some said they were sentient just like people, but no one knew for sure. No one who'd say anyhow.

A few minutes later Lando had some antibiotics in one pocket, Dee's money in another, and her unconscious form over his left shoulder. The gun was in his right hand as he stepped out the door.

The boy was waiting, and a short walk away, so was a taxi. Lando peeled off some more bills, stuffed them into a grubby little hand, and eased Dee into the car. She moaned a little, mumbled something, and lapsed back into unconsciousness.

Like all its kin the auto cab took little notice of its passengers, happy to learn where they were going, and take them there.

The cab rolled through the gates of the spaceport a few

minutes later, and at Lando's request pulled up to a public com booth. Now to answer the big question. Had Sorenson simply deserted them? Or was there some other explanation?

It took twenty-four seconds for Lando's call to route through a comsat and onto *Junk*'s bridge. It was Cap who answered.

"Lando? Is that you? Cy said they took you away somewhere. You'd better get your worthless ass up here! You've got some answering to do!"

Lando smiled. "Yes, sir. I'm on my way."

12

Lando entered the cabin, put the tray on the shelf next to Dee's bunk, and flopped into a chair.

Dee made no response. Her eyes were closed and only the steady rise and fall of her chest indicated that she was alive.

Lando hooked a leg over the arm of the chair. "Cut the crap, Della. About ten minutes ago you were up and around looking for your slug gun."

One eye flew open and glared in his direction. It was very green. "How did you know that?"

Lando pointed up toward the ceiling. "Because shortly after I brought you aboard Cy put a vid pickup on the overhead."

The other eye opened. "You spied on me!"

"We watched to make sure you were okay," Lando countered. "Sorry . . . but we're short on nurses."

Dee sat upright in bed. It hurt but she was too angry to care. "I didn't have any clothes on!"

Lando grinned. "Not true. You had that shirt on. A shirt that happens to be mine by the way."

"But that's all I had on!"

"Now that's true," Lando agreed thoughtfully, "but you should think of me as your doctor."

"My doctor? My doctor?" Dee demanded. "Think of a common criminal as my doctor? No way!"

Lando shrugged. "Have it your way. How're you feeling?"

Dee fell back in bed and turned toward the bulkhead.

Lando got up and headed toward the door. He was halfway through when she spoke.

"Pik . . ."

He turned around. "Yeah?"

"Thanks for taking care of me."

Lando smiled. "I was happy to do it."

Up on *Junk*'s bridge Melissa pushed a button. She made a face as the vid screen faded to black. " 'Thanks for taking care of me.' Oh, think nothing of it, darling, I was happy to do it. Ugh! Absolutely disgusting!" And with that she stomped off the bridge.

Lando knocked on Cap's open door. "You wanted to see me?"

Cap looked up and scowled. Lando saw that while Sorenson hadn't shaved for two days he was reasonably sober. As usual his office was a mess with junk all over the place and a half-empty plate of food by his elbow.

"Yeah, I wanted to see you. You've been avoiding me."

Lando nodded. "True enough. For some strange reason I thought you'd be angry with me."

"Angry with you?" Cap asked sarcastically. "Angry with the man who took my daughter dirtside without permission, dragged her into a gambling den, and got her arrested? Angry? Why would I be angry?"

Lando held up his hands defensively. "Okay, I accept what you're saying. I was wrong to take Melissa dirtside."

"Wrong?" Cap demanded, leaning forward in his chair. " 'Wrong' isn't strong enough. How 'bout stupid? Or criminally insane?

"You knew Cy had a gambling habit, you knew Willer was out there somewhere, you knew about the price on your head . . . I'd say you were something more than 'wrong.' "

Lando's eyes grew narrow. "Why you sanctimonious old bastard. Where the hell were you when Cy and Melissa wanted to go dirtside? I'll tell you where you were, lying unconscious on your bunk, that's where! Melissa is *your* daughter. You want to take care of her? Fine. Stay sober."

Cap's face turned absolutely white. For one long moment both men stared at each other. It was Cap who broke and looked down at the surface of his desk. His voice sounded small.

"You're right of course. I know it doesn't mean much, but

I haven't had a drink since I went to pick her up."

Lando cleared his throat. "It *could* mean something, Cap. It could be a start if you want it to be."

"Yeah," Cap said, looking up and into Lando's eyes. "I guess it could. I've read books about it you know. They say to 'take it one day at a time.' "

Lando nodded. "You could make one little girl extremely happy. And speaking of her, where was she? They split us up early on. Cy and I were worried."

The color returned to Cap's face as he leaned back in his chair. "They took her to some sort of juvenile facility. For a while there I thought I'd have a hard time getting her out, but when I blamed everything on you they released her right away."

Lando grimaced. "Thanks a lot."

"Think nothing of it," Cap replied cheerfully. "Now, Cy was something else again. It turned out that our little friend had gambling debts totaling a quarter million."

"A quarter-million credits?"

"Yup, two hundred and fifty thousand big ones. It took every bit of *your* gold, *my* gold, and the proceeds from the sale of the speedster to pay them off."

"Wait a minute! My gold was hidden!"

"Of course," Cap replied smugly. "But this is *my* ship, remember? I helped build it. It didn't take long to open the ventilation duct, find the gold, and put the screen back in place."

"Why you old . . ."

"Hold on," Cap admonished. "Cy promises to pay us back. Even if he has to stay on my payroll for the next hundred and forty years. Besides, you shouldn't say unpleasant things about the man who lets you bring bounty hunters home, and pays for burned-out rental cars."

"You paid for the rental car?"

Cap nodded. "I had to. Otherwise they were coming up here to take *you* and *your* bounty hunter into custody."

Lando remembered the firefight and the bullets flying every which way. "Thanks, Cap. I'm sorry about the speedster. I know you liked it. When Cy pays me I'll pay you. Or Della will."

Cap gave a grunt. "Thanks. I won't hold my breath. Let's

just finish the contract. It's only a matter of time until Willer comes after us again."

Lando stood up. Cap was right. Willer wanted him dead. As for Cap, well, when it came to the *Star of Empire,* both men were slightly deranged and Willer most of all. He wanted the ship first and Cap second. Were it otherwise Willer could've killed Sorenson a dozen times over. No, he had some sort of crazy fantasy in which Cap would lead him to the ship, the ship that took his body.

"Right. I'll get to work."

"Not so fast," Cap replied. "Take a look at this." He held up a fax.

Lando took it. The fax bore an official-looking seal and was addressed to Cap:

Dear Captain Sorenson,

Regarding the disposition of item D-878 presently occupying OL-18: We are well acquainted with the fact that said item is occupied by unauthorized beings.

However, this fact in no way relieves you or your crew of responsibility for the fulfillment of your contract, and falls within the purview of page sixty-seven, paragraph two, which clearly states " . . . that the contractor shall bear full and complete responsibility for dealing with any and all life forms dwelling in and around such orbital debris during the life of the contract."

With that in mind, we remind you that final payment is conditional upon meeting the agreed-upon deadline, and that your time is nearly up.

Should you dispute the content of this letter please feel free to appeal our decision. Judging by our current caseload your appeal should be heard in six or seven months.

Sincerely yours,

Carolyn Baxter

Secretary, Orbital Commission

Planet of Pylax

Lando handed the letter back. "I don't get it. What 'life forms'? And what is item D-878?"

"It's an old habitat," Cap answered sourly. "I came across it while you were off playing cops and robbers with Lieutenant Itek.

"As I understand it 878 was originally constructed as a small-scale zero-G biological lab. The company that built it went broke, it passed through various hands, and was ultimately abandoned."

"So?"

"So it's too damned big to recycle as is. According to the terms of our contract, we're supposed to break it down into smaller pieces, and that would kill the people living aboard."

Lando raised an eyebrow. "How many people? And how do they survive?"

"Just two," Sorenson replied, "and as for the second part, well, I guess they just sort of scrounge for a living. You know, search for useful debris, steal whatever they can, and so forth."

"So what do you want me to do?"

Cap shrugged. "You read the letter. It's up to us. Either we get rid of them, or we don't get paid. Go over there and evict 'em."

Lando narrowed his eyes suspiciously. "Why me? Why didn't you evict them yourself?"

Sorenson slammed his fist down on the table. It made everything jump. "Because I'm the captain, damn it! Because I own this ship and you don't!"

"Okay, okay," Lando said, moving toward the door. "Don't get yourself in an uproar. Item 878 in OL-18. It's as good as done. See you later."

Lando fired the tender's retros and waited for the ship to match speed with D-878. It certainly wasn't much to look at. A couple of side-by-side cylinders, a long section of grid work that ran at right angles to them, and a mismatched set of solar panels. Cap was right, the damned thing was too big to recycle, and would have to come apart. The sudden squawk of the standard ship-to-ship frequency startled him. The voice was male.

"You there . . . I don't know who you are, or what the hell you're up to, but you'd better get away while the gettin's good.

I have a Nergelon 500 energy cannon aimed your way. One false move and you're free metal."

Lando eyed the habitat's solar panels and checked the tender's sensors. The panels wouldn't generate enough power for a Nergelon 500, and judging from the habitat's heat signature, neither would the small on-board fusion plant. The voice was bluffing.

"All I want is a little conversation," Lando replied. "I'll suit-up and drop over for a visit."

"Don't do that!" the voice replied tersely. "Not unless you want to boil inside your suit!"

"I guess I'll just have to take that chance," Lando replied dryly, and put the tender on standby.

Twenty minutes later Lando was inside his suit and jetting toward the habitat. The suit still smelled like the bottom of a Class IV garbage scow. Lando tried to breathe through his mouth.

D-878 was closer now, close enough to see the main lock, and that's where Lando headed. He was about a hundred yards away when he heard the voice again. This time over his suit radio.

"Okay, I couldn't bring myself to use the energy cannon, but if you board I'll put a blaster bolt through your faceplate!"

"That sounds real messy," Lando replied calmly, "and completely unnecessary. Why not talk instead? That's all I want."

No answer.

Lando flipped end for end and activated the electromagnets in his boots. They hit the cylindrical hull with enough force to bend his knees.

Now that he was right on top of it Lando saw that the habitat was pretty beat-up. It looked as though a ship, or something heavy, had hit one of the cylinders about halfway up. Someone had repaired the gash with a patchwork quilt of roughly joined scrap metal.

There was other damage as well, signs that someone had stripped the hull of external fittings, and been less than gentle in the process.

Lando walked across the hull, grabbed the all-purpose tool from his belt, and rapped on the habitat's lock. He couldn't hear but the people inside the hull could.

No response.

Lando sighed. He chinned the radio on. "Okay, be stubborn. I'll cut my way in."

Lando released the tool and felt the lanyard pull it in. Grabbing the cutting laser that hung at his side, Lando checked to make sure the power pak was fully charged, and flicked it on. The hull metal glowed cherry-red where the beam cut into it.

He felt like the big bad wolf huffing and puffing and blowing the house in.

"All right, all right!" the voice said. "I'll open the lock. Turn that damned thing off. There's enough holes in this pile of junk already."

Lando did as he was told and the lock cycled open. The second he stepped inside it closed behind him as if to keep any others out. Time passed until his external indicator read "Pressure normal, atmosphere breathable." The inner hatch irised open.

Satisfied that they hadn't tried to flood the lock with toxic gas, Lando broke the seals on his suit and pushed his helmet back over his shoulders. The air tasted like the usual recycled stuff. Killing the power to his boots Lando launched himself toward the hatch. Arriving outside he expected the voice would be there to greet him. Outside of a beat-up old space suit on a rack, and a net full of salvaged junk, there was no sign of another human being.

Lando pulled himself through a hatch and into a long corridor. In spite of the cracked and dirty paint, he could make out the words "Crew Quarters" stenciled on the bulkhead, along with a faded green arrow.

Using conveniently placed handholds to pull himself along, Lando saw that the floor of the tunnel was almost as good as new. Without argrav nobody had ever used it. Of course "floor" was a somewhat relative term in zero G but it seemed to fit because the path in question was free of conduit and equipped with a plastic mat.

Now a solid bulkhead blocked Lando's way. It had a hatch but that had been welded shut. The faded sign said "Crew Quarters" but a crudely drawn arrow pointed toward the left.

Lando opened a small access door and followed, realizing that he was inside a maintenance tunnel, and moving from one cylinder to the next. The passageway was dark but Lando saw light up ahead.

A few moments later he swam out and into a relatively large compartment. It had once served the lab as both cafeteria and lounge. Now it looked like a somewhat messy apartment. There was stuff all over the place, most of it secured by nets, but some floating free.

And there right in the middle of the room was an old man, and behind him in some sort of hammock affair was an elderly woman. Lando couldn't be sure what with the blankets and so forth but it looked as though her body was twisted by some sort of terrible disease. The hammock made a sort of free-floating nest in which she could rest pressure-free.

She looked like a fragile bird, with small features and a nose just a shade too large for her face. There was something in her eyes though, a brightness, which made her beautiful. In spite of Lando's uninvited status she smiled and the pilot found himself smiling back.

The man was thin, with a halo of white hair around an otherwise bald head, and deep circles under his eyes. As Lando approached, he moved to place himself in front of the woman. The man was scared but determined. The blaster shook slightly in his hand. "That's far enough! Now, what do you want?"

Lando smiled disarmingly. "Hi, my name's Pik Lando. I work aboard a salvage tug, and we . . ."

"I already told the first guy no," the old man said, "we aren't leaving the lab. My wife's sick and if I take her dirtside she'll die. We can't afford a zero-G hospital so I brought her here. It took all our savings just to make the habitat livable. So do your worst."

"Now, Herbert . . ." the woman started.

"No, Edith, I mean it," Herbert replied sternly. "We've been through this a dozen times. This is our home now. It's as good a place as any to die."

Lando sighed. He'd been royally had. Cap had been here, found himself unable to evict the elderly squatters, and sent someone else to do his dirty work. Well, it wasn't going to happen. He forced a smile.

"Sorry to impose on you folks. I'll be on my way."

Lando was just about to enter the maintenance tunnel when Herbert stopped him. "Wait a minute, young man . . . what are you going to do?"

Lando looked around. "Beats me, Herbert. But whatever it is won't hurt you or Edith."

The blaster wavered and dropped. "I'm sorry about the threats. We were scared."

Lando nodded soberly. "That's quite all right. You take care. I'll see you later."

"We'll be here." Herbert put his arm around Edith's shoulders and she smiled.

The image of Edith's loving face and Herbert's fierce determination was still clear in Lando's mind when he reached *Junk*.

He headed straight for Cap's cabin and didn't knock when he entered. Cap looked up from his com screen. "Well? Did you kick 'em out?"

Lando was angry. "No, I didn't 'kick them out.' And neither did you!"

Cap shrugged. "I don't have to. I have you to do those things for me. You know the score. Either we move 'em or we don't get paid."

Lando was just about to speak, to tell Cap what a worthless lowlife he was, when something clicked. "What did you say?"

Cap raised an eyebrow. "I said, 'You know the score . . . either we move 'em or we don't get paid.' You're starting to slip, Lando. Maybe that pressor beam scrambled your brains."

Lando ignored the insult. "Move 'em! That's the answer!"

Cap leaned back and shook his head. " 'Fraid not. I thought of that one too. Use *Junk* to tow 'em into a different orbit. Nice thought but it won't work. We agreed to clean things up, not just move them from one orbit to another."

Lando shook his head. "That's not what I meant. We've got some portable thrusters right? The heavy-duty jobs you sometimes mount on big tows? We could strap a few of those on the lab!"

Cap frowned. "So what good would that do? It's like I told you. Moving the lab isn't enough."

"No," Lando said impatiently, "you don't understand. Think about it. What's the difference between a habitat and a ship?"

Cap looked thoughtful. "Well, a habitat stays in orbit and a ship has the capability to"—the older man's face lit up with sudden understanding—"travel from place to place! That's great!" Then his face fell. "Damn."

"What?"

"It won't work, Lando. Sure, the thrusters might get them to another planet, but they might not too. All kinds of things could go wrong. Chances are we'd send them to their deaths."

Lando smiled. "Wrong, Cap, you still don't get it. Like you said, a ship has the *capability* to travel, and that means that it falls outside the authority of the Commission. They can levy a parking fee but that's it."

Cap nodded slowly. "I'll have to check but I think you're right. But what about the cost? Those thrusters are worth a thousand credits apiece, and how 'bout the parking fees?"

Lando paused in the doorway and smiled. "Think about it, Cap. Which would you rather have? The money or a clear conscience?"

Cap scowled. "The money."

But he didn't mean it, and three rotations later it was he who poured champagne on the lab's durasteel deck, and named her after a flightless bird. And light sparkled off mismatched solar panels as the good ship *Penguin* circled the planet Pylax.

13

"You can't be serious!" Everyone was there, Lando, Cap, Melissa, Cy, and Dee. Cap had summoned them to the bridge for a 'crew meeting' but it sounded like an announcement. Lando was on his feet, hands clenched at his side.

Cap looked straight ahead. His features were rigid. Light from the vid screens gave his skin a greenish pallor. "Yes I can! Try to get this through your head, Lando, this is more than a place for you to hide, it's a *business*. And unless this business brings in some money, and damned soon, *Junk* goes on the auction block."

"But, Daddy," Melissa objected, climbing onto a power supply console, "Jord Willer hates you! He tried to kill Pik! You shouldn't trust him!"

"I don't trust him," her father replied grimly. "And how many times have I asked you to get off that console?"

Sorenson turned toward Lando. "The simple fact is that we need the money. This is the best tow we've had in a long time and I think it's safe. Willer works for Stellar Tug & Salvage and they're hiring us. It seems all of their other tugs are busy. There's two barges, more than the *Hercules* can handle alone, so Willer needs our help. If he hurts us, he hurts himself."

"Maybe," Lando said doubtfully, "but you're acting as though Willer's a rational being. What if he freaks out?"

Cap shrugged. "Then we'll deal with it. Meanwhile we take the tow. The course is in the NAVCOMP. Get us there." And with that Sorenson walked off the bridge.

All of them watched him go, then turned to look at each other. All except for Melissa who did her best to ignore Della

Dee and looked at Lando instead. "Daddy hasn't been sick in a long time."

"Yeah," Lando agreed, "he's doing very well. Would you fetch me a cup of coffee from the galley?"

Melissa jumped down from the power supply console. "You want me to leave so you can talk grown-up stuff," she said wisely. "Why didn't you just say so?" and skipped off toward the starboard lift tube.

Lando looked at the other two. "So what do you think?"

Cy bobbed gently as the recycler came on and blew air at him from a nearby vent. "Maybe Cap's right. It's a big tow. Maybe Willer *will* put grudges aside and concentrate on the task at hand."

"And maybe the Emp will name you his ambassador to New Britain," Dee scoffed. "I saw the bastard from the wrong end of a shotgun. He's crazy, and that's all there is to it."

Lando nodded his agreement. "I think Della's right, and even if she isn't, it doesn't hurt to be prepared. Let's make a plan."

It took another day and a half to reach the pickup point. Like most utility worlds IW-67 was something less than pretty. First there was a soupy atmosphere made mostly of pollutants. Then came a scabrous surface pitted with strip mines. The older ones had become lakes of semisolid waste, open sores from which deathly brown rivers flowed, slowly oozing toward seas of undulating black goo.

Seas that were home to bottom-dwelling robo-miners, vast crawlers that inched their way across the ocean floors and ate everything of value.

In essence the world was a corpse full of mechanical maggots. Each day the maggots ate their fill, gave birth to even more maggots, and expelled tons of poisonous waste. Eventually, when the corpse had nothing left to give, it would be abandoned and the maggots would move elsewhere.

No one objected, no one cared, because outside of a thousand or so contract workers no one lived on IW-67. What little native life there was had been sampled, declared useless, and allowed to die.

Could some of it have evolved? Grown to sentience? Launched spacecraft and traveled to distant stars? No one would ever know.

Such were the ways of the huge mega-corporations that made the things people wanted to have.

It reminded Lando of Angel, the planet on which he and others had battled one such corporation, and won. But not IW-67. Its death was already certain and it was his job to help strip the corpse.

Lando saw two barges and a tug with his sensors long before he saw them with his eyes.

The barges were huge, twice as big as a battleship, and shaped more like cylindrical tanks than rectangular "barges."

Both were loaded with chlorine that had been manufactured on IW-67's surface and boosted into orbit with a nuclear catapult.

The catapult consisted of a half-mile deep hole, a pulsing reactor, and a supply of reinforced containers. Shove the containers down the hole, set off the nuclear explosion, and, presto, about twenty thousand miles later the cargo was in orbit. Crude, but effective, and perfect for a world where no one cared about radiation.

Once in orbit the chlorine was transferred from the launch modules to the huge gas barges. And since the tankers had no propulsion systems of their own, they must be towed to their final destination. That was *Junk*'s task.

Lando triggered the intercom. "Barges in sight. Prepare ship for maneuvers and tow."

"Roger," Cy replied from *Junk*'s engineering section. "All systems are in the green."

"Coming," Cap grunted from his stateroom. "I'll be on the bridge five from now."

"No problems here," Melissa said cheerfully. "Lunch will consist of gucky green nutra-paste on gray crackers with dried fruit on the side."

"Sounds tempting," Lando replied, "I can hardly wait."

Melissa giggled while he scanned the screens. The cylinders were larger now, each showing up as a three-dimensional cigar and emitting its own unique radio signal.

And then there was Jord Willer's ship *Hercules,* an arrow-shaped chunk of red, surrounded by a yellow-orange heat blob, and emanating a rainbow of color-coded signals. Just looking at it scared the daylights out of him.

Lando touched a button. "Della?"

"Yeah?"

"We're coming up on *Hercules*. Time to step outside."

"I read you," Dee answered. "E-lock four cycling now."

Emergency-lock four had been chosen with great care. For one thing it was located on the side of the hull away from *Hercules* and prying eyes. In spite of that however Della's mission could still be extremely dangerous. Lando was worried.

"Della?"

"Yeah?"

"You be careful out there."

"I will . . . you too."

The words left a lot unsaid. Thanks to a hardy constitution and the attentions of the robot doctor, Dee's wounds were completely healed. So, while she was free to go, the bounty hunter had chosen to stay aboard. She was short of funds, that's true, but there was something else too, something she and Lando were just starting to explore.

Both were loners by inclination and necessity, slow to enter new relationships, but willing to consider all the possibilities. If asked, both would deny special affection for the other, but the feelings were there, and clear for others to see. Especially Melissa, who felt Dee was taking increasing amounts of Lando's attention, and had few qualms about making her resentment known.

So while Dee continued to refer to Lando as "money in the bank," and he to her as "an Imperial vulture," neither did anything to change the way things were.

As a result Dee had become a de facto member of the crew, earning wages, and waiting to see what would happen.

Having no real ship-related skills, and being a bounty hunter, Dee was the logical choice for her current assignment and had volunteered. Besides, given the fact that they couldn't tell Cap what she was up to, Dee was the only person available.

A buzzer buzzed and an indicator light came on. Dee was outside the ship and climbing aboard her sled. It was loaded with extra fuel and oxygen. Enough to last days if necessary. Her suit would provide everything else.

The comset beeped and a screen came to life. Lando looked up into the perfect features of Jord Willer.

• • •

Dee forced herself to wait. Lando had stressed the importance of that. He would pass as close to *Hercules* as he could. Then, for one brief moment the heat and electromagnetic activity generated by both ships would be all jumbled together, and Dee would make her move.

Standing up to peer over the dark curvature of *Junk*'s hull she could see the other tug hurtling toward her. Although neither ship was moving very fast their combined speeds amounted to more than a thousand miles an hour.

The space suit felt awkward and heavy as Dee sat down and released the sled's magnetic locks. It smelled funny too, like someone she didn't know, and didn't want to.

The sled was little more than a metal framework with some thrusters, two seats, and room for cargo in the back. All the comforts of home.

Junk seemed to leap out from under her as the sled floated free. Dee fought to orient herself as IW-67 filled her vision with reflected light. Where was *Hercules*? The damned thing had disappeared. No, wait a minute, there it was. Almost here!

Light winked off the ship's bow as it blocked part of the planet below. She had to leave now while the jumble of heat and electronic emissions would cover her movements.

Dee fired her thrusters and aimed her tiny craft at the ship's broad back. It came up fast, a virtual forest of weapons blisters, beam projectors, and other installations each waiting to rip her apart.

Killing thrust, Dee fired the sled's retros and grit her teeth. Maybe Pik could put the sled down wherever he wanted to but in her case it would be pure luck. Rather than admit her lack of expertise Dee had allowed him to assume more experience than she actually had.

There . . . if she could only land in that clear space just aft of the central cooling fin . . . The sled hit with a solid thump that bounced her head off the padding inside her helmet. Damn! The landing must have made a god-awful clang inside the tug's hull. Had anyone heard?

"So," Willer said, "we meet again."

Once again Lando was struck by the cyborg's unnatural

beauty. The blond hair, the flawless features, the perfectly modulated voice. He forced a smile.

"Hi, Willer. I guess some things never change. You still look ugly as hell."

"And that's enough of that," Cap said sternly as he dropped into the chair on Lando's right. "Hello, Jord. I apologize for my pilot."

Willer smiled. "Hello, Captain. Apology accepted. One of these days your pilot and I will settle our differences. This is neither the time nor the place. There's a job to do and I suggest we do it."

Cap gave Lando a look that had "I told you so" written all over it, and turned back to the screen.

"I agree. The contract puts you in command. How can we help?"

Lando thought he saw a glint of satisfaction deep in the cyborg's eyes but he could've been wrong. Perhaps it was light reflecting off his artificial pupils.

"Our first task is to join the barges together. It's been my experience that one tow is easier to deal with than two."

Cap nodded his agreement.

"Once that's accomplished," Willer continued, "my ship will take the lead, with *Junk* pushing from behind. Questions?"

"Yeah," Lando answered. "Who's in charge of linking the barges together?"

Light reflected off Willer's teeth. "I'll ask Captain Sorenson to handle that little chore."

Cap swallowed but kept his voice steady. "I'll be glad to."

"Excellent," Willer replied. "Let me know when you're in position." And with that the screen faded to black.

Cap stood and turned to go. Lando touched his arm.

"Don't do it, Cap. The bastard's up to something."

Sorenson pulled his arm away. "Give it a rest, Lando. You heard him. We have a job to do. If we do our part he'll do his. I'll call you from the lock." And with that he walked away.

Lando turned back to his screens. Chances were the other man was right. Chances were everything was fine. And chances were that pigs could fly.

• • •

Dee waited five long minutes and heaved a sigh of relief. Maybe the landing was quieter than she thought, or maybe no one had heard, but whatever the case it seemed she was in the clear. Checking to make sure that the sled was securely clamped to the ship's hull, Dee made a place for herself among the extra O_2 tanks, and settled down to wait. The suit hummed around her.

"Okay, Lando, I'm on barge one."

Lando could just barely see Cap on high mag. He was standing on what momentarily passed for the top surface of barge one, right next to one of the huge docking clamps.

"That's a rog, Cap. I have you on visual. *Junk* to *Hercules*. Captain Sorenson is in place."

"We copy," Willer's voice came back. "Lock some beams on barge two. Your job is to hold it steady while we push barge one into place."

Lando was soon lost in the task at hand. First there was the need to place *Junk* in the proper position. That required precise use of the big side thrusters and smaller steering jets.

Once the ship was in place the tractor and pressor beams came into play. Lando pushed them out, made contact, and locked on. He was fine-tuning them when Cap's voice came over the comset.

"Lando, watch out! Barge one's coming your way!"

Lando looked up at the starboard vid screen and was horrified. Barge one had come adrift somehow and was moving toward him. It already filled the screen and would hit sometime within the next sixty seconds. The barge was huge, and even though it didn't have much weight, it still packed a lot of inertia. It could crush the tug and keep right on going.

Lando's fingers darted here and there. Beams were severed, thrusters were fired, and *Junk* lurched upward. The ship shuddered and metal groaned as hulls made momentary contact. Then the barge was gone and they were clear.

Now that he had a moment to think, Lando understood Willer's plan. With the ships working so close together the cyborg *knew* Lando would defeat the collision alarms, *knew* he'd be lost in the task before him, and thought the plan would work.

So with Cap riding on top, the cyborg had pushed barge one toward *Junk*, and sat back to watch. If things went well, Cap would not only *see* the destruction, he'd be *part* of it, and still survive to help find the *Star of Empire*.

Thank Sol that Cap had been sober and paying attention. The plan had come close to working.

The com screen lit up. It was Willer. His face bore an expression of mock concern. "Nice work, Lando. Sorry about that. One of my people lost control for a moment. No harm done I hope?"

Lando grabbed the armrests to keep his hands from shaking. Cap tried to say something on the suit-to-suit freq but the pilot cut him off.

"Cut the crap, Willer. You tried and failed. Now you pay."

"Oh, really?" Willer sneered. "And what will you do? Shoot at us with one of your popguns? The *Hercules* can match you weapon for weapon and then some."

"True as far as it goes," Lando answered tightly. "But we've got a little surprise for you. Della, give him a demo."

This was the signal Dee had been waiting for. A chance to even the score if only a little. She brought the blast rifle up to her shoulder. A large vid cam filled the sights. She pressed the FIRE button and watched the lance of bright blue energy slice through the camera's flat-black housing.

Two things happened in quick succession. The screen that provided Willer with coverage of the tug's port side went black, and as it did, he activated the ship's protective force field.

Lando laughed. "Nice try, chrome dome, but you've got a flea on your mangy hide, and all the force fields in the world won't help you."

Della dialed the rifle to WIDE BEAM and cooked a VHF antenna. It turned cherry-red and drooped like an overcooked noodle.

A buzzer went off and a light flashed red on Willer's control console. He swore a blue streak. Lando had someone on the hull! Someone inside the force field and therefore too close to hit with the tug's armament. Not only that, they were systematically blinding his ship!

Another vid screen dumped to black and Willer smashed his metal hand down and through the surface of the control board.

Sparks flew, something started to burn, and smoke poured into the control room.

Willer's pilot, a somewhat slovenly looking woman with a dope stick dangling from her lower lip, shook her head, but kept her own counsel. She'd never seen the borg this angry before.

"You'll pay for this, Lando! I'll kill her and come for you!"

Lando nodded sympathetically. "Good thinking, space head. Go ahead and suit-up. Della would like that. She's a bounty hunter by profession. You know, the one you shot in the chest, and she wants you *real* bad. Isn't that right, Della?"

Della answered by cooking another vid cam.

Willer screamed his rage and ordered his crew into their suits. "Get out there! Kill her! Do it now!"

No one answered. Willer turned to his pilot and found she wasn't there. The crew had no intention of going one on one with a bounty hunter, especially when she could wait right outside the lock and nail them as they left.

This made the cyborg even more furious. He went on a rampage smashing anything that got in his way and adding to the already extensive damage.

And finally, when fatigue had overcome his rage, Willer found that his ship was blind. Dee had systematically located and destroyed every vid cam, every sensor, and every antenna she could find, leaving nothing but one short-range ship-to-ship com link. The humiliation was almost more than the cyborg could bear. It took him the better part of an hour to make contact.

"You made your point, Lando. This round goes to you. But I'll find you, and when I do, you're dead!"

"I love you too," Lando said easily. "Now listen up. We're going to finish the tow. Kill your force field, place your control systems on standby, and slave your NAVCOMP to ours. We'll take it from there."

And they did. It took longer, and was damned awkward at times, but they did it. With *Junk* performing all the close-quarters maneuvering, and *Hercules* providing brute strength, the cylinders were linked and towed into orbit around Pylax.

In order to keep Willer and his crew from making repairs Dee was forced to ride the ship's hull for most of the trip. It was nerve-wracking sleepless duty, and she was completely exhausted by the time the trip was over, but it was worth it.

Not only had Dee achieved some measure of revenge, she had also proved her worth as a member of *Junk*'s crew, and earned Lando's respect on top of that. Something the bounty hunter didn't even know she wanted until she had it.

By unspoken agreement Cap and Lando never discussed why Dee had taken up a position on the other ship's hull or who was right about Willer.

Both shared a concern that Willer might file charges against them, charges they could refute using tapes of what had transpired, but charges that would immobilize *Junk* for weeks or even months.

Maybe Willer knew he couldn't win a legal battle, or maybe he preferred to have his revenge in other more direct ways, but whatever the reason charges were never filed.

And they never did learn what sort of story Willer concocted for his company. But it didn't matter. What mattered was that the company paid them off, *Junk* was momentarily in the black, and her crew had a reason to party. With that in mind they were gathered on the bridge.

Cap held up his glass of fruit juice. Melissa did likewise, as did Lando and Dee, while Cy prepared to release a tiny amount of alcohol into the nutrient solution around his brain. "To a motley crew, a ship named *Junk,* and the luck that holds them all together!"

They looked at each other, laughed, and repeated in unison: "To a motley crew, a ship named *Junk,* and the luck that holds them all together!"

14

The *Princess Claudia* was one of the largest, most luxurious liners in existence. Rivaled only by her sister ship, the *Prince Alexander,* she had one and only one purpose: to transport the empire's wealthiest passengers from one place to another in absolute luxury. And she was equipped to do the job.

The *Claudia*'s huge drives could take her from one end of the empire to the other at incredible speed. She had backup systems for her backup systems, an empire-class galley, hundreds of luxurious staterooms, and the best crew money could buy.

It was not surprising therefore that her main banquet room was both large and opulent. The room was circular in shape, which echoed the ship's globular design, and allowed for a unique seating arrangement.

The tables were arranged in a series of concentric rings, with the less affluent passengers on the outside, and the downright rich toward the center. There were fifty tables in all, each seated eight bejeweled guests, and was served by two sentient waiters. The centermost table, the one located directly under the enormous chandelier of pink Edon rock crystal, belonged to *Claudia*'s commanding officer.

Captain Naomi Neubeck pushed herself away from the linen-covered table. She'd done it again, eaten way more than she should've, and Bones would give her hell. With her annual physical just two months away Neubeck needed to drop some weight but had put it off. Even in the low shipboard gravity she could feel the fat weighing her down. She'd work on it tomorrow.

Neubeck smiled at the men and women who lined her table. All had the rosy glow that comes with a mega-credit income, a twelve-course dinner, and some extremely good wine.

"Thank you for joining my table. Please enjoy the rest of the cruise and let me know if there's anything we can do to make the trip more pleasant."

Neubeck waved off the chorus of "thank you's," and headed for her day cabin. It was a comfortable ritual and rarely varied.

Have dinner with some of her rich passengers, make a final entry in her log, and call the bridge. Utter some sympathetic noises as Second Officer Rubashkin slandered the engineering staff, check the ship's position, and leave some orders for the next watch. Then it was down the hall to her sleeping cabin for a full nine hours of sleep. She couldn't wait.

Hu was a small man, with straight black hair and intelligent brown eyes. He knew Rubashkin was on duty, knew the second officer hated engineering, and knew how the conversation would go.

"Bridge . . . Rubashkin speaking."

"This is Hu. We have a problem."

"That's for sure. Tell me something I didn't already know."

Hu bit his lower lip and tried to keep his temper. "Our computer shows abnormal wear on field projector three. It's going to fail sometime during the next four or five hours. We can replace it now or wait for the projector to go belly up."

Rubashkin was silent while he thought it over. At the moment they were looping around Durna preparatory to entering hyperspace on the other side. The engineers would be forced to shut down the ship's protective force field in order to replace projector three.

Running the force field full-time sucked up a lot of energy, and added to operating expense, but provided an extra margin of safety in the unlikely event of a pirate attack or collision. Just one of the many things that put the Empire Line a cut above all the rest.

Still, the way Hu explained the situation, there was no way to win. Lose the field now, or lose it later. Not much of a choice with a hyperspace jump coming up and an irritable captain asleep below. The whole crew would celebrate when Neubeck passed her physical.

For one brief moment Rubashkin considered waking Neubeck to ask her opinion but quickly put the thought aside. No, she wouldn't appreciate being woken up, plus she'd give him the promotion lecture.

"How will you make first officer if you pass the buck? Show some backbone, Rubashkin . . . make a decision."

He hated that lecture almost as much as the one Bones gave on sexual hygiene.

"Go ahead and take the field down," Rubashkin said. "But work fast . . . otherwise I'll have your ass for breakfast!"

"Yes, sir," Hu replied sweetly, "and I hope you'll feel free to kiss it in the meantime." The engineer broke the connection before Rubashkin could reply.

The meteor was round but not perfectly so. It consisted of iron, nickel, and traces of other minerals. The meteor had been traveling around Durna for millions of years. During its lifetime planets had hardened, ecosystems had been born, and entire species had been plunged into extinction. It neither knew nor cared.

The odds against the meteor and the *Princess Claudia* trying to occupy the same space at the same time were unbelievably huge. And the odds of this happening during the brief period in which the liner's force field was down and the ship was in close proximity to the system's sun were even larger, but that's what happened.

The meteor was traveling at about twenty-six miles per second when it hit the *Princess Claudia* and sliced through the liner's durasteel hull like a knife through warm butter.

As luck would have it, the meteor followed the line of the ship's axis, holing both in-line drives and seventeen previously airtight compartments in the process.

Fifty-six men, women, and children died instantly. Twelve of them were engineers and one of those was Hu. During the next few hours another fourteen would die of wounds suffered during those few seconds.

The effect was almost instantaneous. Acting on the information provided by thousands of on-board sensors the ship's computer closed airtight doors, shunted all remaining power to essential systems, and set off a cacophony of alarms. One of these was right next to Neubeck's head. She rolled over and stabbed a button.

"Neubeck here . . . what's the problem?"

Second Officer Rubashkin's voice was tight. "We've been holed, Captain, reamed is more like it, damned near the whole length of the ship. Early reports suggest a meteor."

"It went right through the force field?"

Rubashkin felt his throat constrict. Poor Hu. He wanted to throw up. "It was my fault, Captain. The number three force field projector was on its way out. I authorized repairs."

Neubeck was struggling into her uniform. "Don't blame yourself, Andre. I would've made the same decision. Casualties?"

"Heavy I'm afraid," Rubashkin answered. "Hold one. Tell 'em to seal it off! We'll get a damage control party down there as soon as we can!

"Sorry, Captain, we've got a fire in the Purser's Office, electrical probably. We'll dump power to that location, pump the air out, and deal with it later."

Neubeck ran a brush through her hair. "Do you see an immediate need to abandon?"

Rubashkin paused for a second as if thinking it over. "Nah, it's not that bad, Captain, at least not yet."

Neubeck let out her breath. "Thank Sol. Good work, Andre. I'm on my way."

"Authority rests partly on appearance," that's what they teach you at the Imperial Maritime Academy, and it's definitely true.

Neubeck looked in the mirror. A rather plump middle-aged woman with prematurely gray hair looked back. Where had the extra chin come from? Damn. She'd start the diet tomorrow, but for the moment this body would have to do.

Neubeck stepped out of the cabin and into chaos. The emergency lights provided just enough illumination to see by, a recorded announcement insisted that passengers stay right where they were, and the air smelled faintly of smoke. Thank Sol the argrav was still operational. The passengers were frightened enough without floating around in zero G.

A cadet ran toward her, one of six young men and women in training to become officers, and not a day over sixteen. He held something in his arms and wore a look of wide-eyed desperation. Neubeck grabbed his arm and forced him to stop.

"Tolan."

"Yes, ma'am?"

"Walk, don't run. Remember, the passengers and crew are looking to you for an example. Understand?"

Tolan stood a little taller. "Yes, ma'am!"

"Good. Carry on."

Neubeck forced herself to follow her own advice as she strolled down the corridor.

"Citizen Tanaka, good to see you. Yes, everything's okay, please return to your stateroom."

"Lady Carolyn, what a stunning robe! Why don't you step back inside? I wouldn't want it damaged."

"Technician Quigley . . . you're supposed to be on C deck standing by the emergency fusion plant, are you not? Kindly go there without further delay. Walk don't run, Quigley . . . this is an Empire liner after all."

And so it went until Neubeck reached the bridge. It was huge and, given the ship's considerable status, appropriately impressive. No less than twenty-six large screens covered the curved bulkheads. Some were ominously blank.

Three of them showed a ragged hole in the *Claudia*'s hull, surprisingly small for all the damage it had done, and leaking a column of whitish vapor.

Below the screens, control panels glowed, each containing hundreds of green, red, and amber buttons, each controlling and monitoring an important part of the ship.

You could almost tell where the problems were by the number of people gathered around each station. Hydroponics was unmanned, while a small army was clustered around the engineering station, and damage control was double teamed.

Neubeck climbed the two steps to her thronelike command chair and dropped in. It sank slightly and adjusted to her form.

Due to the emergency there were more rather than less people on the bridge. Officers and technicians from all three watches had shown up and were trying to help. It was interesting to see how each reacted to stress.

Many seemed unaffected but here and there Neubeck saw definite changes.

A normally calm power tech shouted into his intercom as if the volume of his voice could get him what he needed. And there, over on the other side of the bridge, the usually dour fourth officer was cracking jokes like a professional comedian.

It was quite a show but she had little time to appreciate it. The moment the bridge crew realized Neubeck was there everyone spoke at once.

"Which do you want more, Captain? Argrav or power to the force field?"

"The passengers are worried, Captain . . . there's a mob forming on the boat deck."

"The fire's out in the Purser's Office . . . she wants to know if we'll repressurize. The passengers want their valuables."

"Silence!" The voice belonged to Rubashkin and it had the desired effect.

Neubeck put on her smile, the professional one which said, "I'm confident and you should be too." She gave her orders in a crisp, calm voice.

"Hold your questions until asked. First things first. All personnel not actually part of this watch to the rear of the bridge. You'll be called on as needed."

Ten or twelve people headed for the rear of the bridge.

"Andre . . . how much power on the drives?"

Rubashkin was a big burly man, with beady little brown eyes and a thick black beard. There were circles of sweat under both his arms.

"None, Captain. The meteor hit both drives. We could shunt some power from the fusion plant to the auxiliary thrusters, but it wouldn't do much good."

Neubeck swallowed hard. None! It seemed hard to believe. "How about repairs?"

Rubashkin shook his head sadly. "The engineering spaces got the worst of it. The meteor killed all of our engineering officers and seventy percent of the techs. The survivors say that drive one is completely hopeless. As for drive two, well, they aren't sure. Repairs would take the supervision of a competent engineer."

Neubeck's eyes went to the main screen. Durna filled it with her fiery presence. Could she actually see the sun getting larger or was that just her imagination? She cleared her throat. "How long before Durna pulls us down?"

Rubashkin shrugged. "Forty, maybe fifty hours."

Damn! They would have to take a hit right on the edge of the sun's gravity well.

Neubeck shifted her gaze to the nav screen. It showed the entire Durna system, including the asteroid belt, Dista, Pylax, and the other mostly uninhabited planets. They needed assistance and needed it fast. "You called for help?"

"First thing," Com Tech Formo answered. She was small, with severe bangs and an elfin face. "I looped a distress call. Still no answer."

Neubeck nodded understandingly. They were a long ways out. Still, Durna was a well-populated system, and they should hear something soon. "All right. Let me know the minute you get a response."

Neubeck turned to Rubashkin. "It sounds like the passengers are getting restless. How many did we lose?"

Rubashkin examined a printout. "Fourteen. Due to the point of penetration the meteor killed more crew than passengers."

Neubeck nodded her understanding. "Gather all the friends and family into one place. B lounge would do nicely. Get the chaplain down there. Whatever you do, keep 'em away from the rest. Grief breeds panic.

"How 'bout the main banquet room? Any damage?"

Rubashkin glanced at the fourth officer and got a shake of the head. "No damage, Captain. Why?"

"Call the galley. Tell them to prepare for a party. Get a hold of the chief steward. Tell him to notify the passengers. They have one hour to prepare for a costume ball. A thousand credits for the most attractive outfit. Once you have them in the main banquet room make sure they stay there until further orders."

Rubashkin smiled at Neubeck's plan and turned away to give the appropriate orders.

Neubeck motioned to the fourth officer. He stepped over. His name was Arthur Zembey and in place of the frown he normally wore there was a smile. "Good evening, Captain. Have a nice nap?"

Neubeck smiled in return. "Somewhat shorter than I would've liked, Arthur, but it'll do. Where's number one?"

The first officer was a woman named Indulo and should've been on the bridge by now.

"Unconscious," Zembey replied. "She led a damage control party into drive room one. Something came loose and bounced her head off the inside of her helmet."

Neubeck swore silently. Indulo was a real loss. Well, one had to make do. "Listen carefully, Arthur. I want you to coordinate all damage control. Get a patch on the hull. Repressurize the damaged compartments as soon as you can. Seal drive room one and forget it. Do what you can for drive room two. Have it ready for repairs. Sift the passenger list for engineers. Maybe we'll luck out. Sol knows we deserve it!

"Have the pilot run a computer projection. How long can we wait before launching the boats? Meanwhile hide all the damage you can. It hurts morale. And have someone get me a cup of coffee, but make it black, I'm on a diet."

Zembey gave Neubeck a salute along with a big grin. The captain was going on her annual diet! The ship would live! He hurried off to execute his orders and spread the news.

As the fourth officer departed, Neubeck felt her eyes drawn to Durna. It filled the main screen like the mouth of a hungry furnace just waiting to grab her ship and pull it down. For the first time since the meteor hit she felt really scared.

15

Lando liked exercise, the *real* kind, which involves some sort of accomplishment. If there was anything more boring than walking on a treadmill he couldn't think of what it was. Walking was boring, the gray little compartment was boring, and his thoughts were boring.

On the other hand, *not* being in shape was even worse, so he did it anyway. Melissa was a welcome interruption.

She entered the gym like a cyclone, jumped onto the treadmill, and walked backward. She wore a big grin. "I know something you don't."

Lando used a towel to wipe the sweat off his forehead. "Good. I hope it's some math."

Melissa produced an exaggerated pout. "That's not fair! I'm doing very well. You said so yourself!"

Lando snapped the towel in her direction and she jumped off the treadmill. "Sure, but 'very well' and 'outstanding' are two different things."

Melissa made a face and stuck out her tongue. "For the next few days I'll be too busy to study math."

"Why's that?"

" 'Cause we've got a tow that's why. A big one."

A timer went off. Lando stepped off the treadmill. Sensing his absence the machine turned itself off. "A tow, huh? How do you know?"

Melissa jumped up, grabbed the chinning bar, and swung back and forth. "I know because I was on the bridge when the call came in." She dropped to the padded deck with a small thump.

"In fact . . . Daddy should call right about now."

So saying Melissa assumed a dramatic pose and pointed toward the intercom. It bonged right on cue. She smiled triumphantly as Lando shook his head in pretended amazement.

"Lando here."

Cap sounded tense. "We've got a tow, Lando . . . a big one. I need you on the bridge."

"Coming," Lando answered, and chased Melissa down the corridor toward the lift tubes. She won as always.

They arrived on the bridge to find everyone else already there. Cap was seated in front of the NAVCOMP typing away, Dee was slouched behind the weapons control module, and Cy hovered in midair.

"What's up?"

Lando dropped into the seat next to Dee. She wore a tight ship-suit and he liked the view. Dee knew it and smiled.

Cap answered without turning around. "We received a distress call from an Empire liner called the *Princess Claudia.*"

Lando gave a low whistle. "The *Princess Claudia.* The biggest and the best. What's the problem?"

"A meteor strike," Cap answered. "It punched a hole through her hull and disabled both drives."

"What about her force field?" Cy asked. "I thought the big liners ran 'em full-time."

"Normally they do," Cap answered, "unfortunately theirs was down for repairs. A meteor happened along, and whamo."

Dee shook her head sympathetically. "Rotten luck."

"Yeah," Cap agreed distractedly. "But that's not the worst of it. They were pretty close in when the accident happened. Bit by bit they're falling into the sun."

Lando was on his feet. "Into Durna? How long do we have?"

Cap pushed a button that shunted the NAVCOMP's output over to the main screen. Lando saw the system, a projected course that would carry them dangerously close to the sun, and a digital readout. It read forty-one hours, sixteen minutes, and thirty-two seconds. As he watched the two changed to a one.

Cap turned around. His voice was grim. "During the next thirty minutes *Junk* will accelerate to maximum speed. Even so it will take eighteen hours to get there, and by the time we put some tractor beams on her, the *Claudia* may have fallen too far for us to tow her alone. Even the most optimistic computer projections say we'll be lucky to hold the ship where she is. In fact, given her mass and Durna's gravity, she could pull us down with her."

"How 'bout other tugs?" Cy inquired. "This is a rich tow. In fact, since she has no power of her own, we can claim salvage. Surely they want a piece of the action?"

Cap nodded soberly. "You bet they do . . . but we're closest . . . and they won't arrive until the critical moment has passed."

Lando returned his attention to the main screen. Cap was right. They were the only ones who could help. With some money in the bank, and the crew paid up, Sorenson had resumed his search for the *Star of Empire*. He'd paid good money for those coordinates and planned to use 'em.

As a result *Junk* was halfway to the asteroid belt when the distress call came in, a location that put her closer to the sun than the other tugs happened to be, and best positioned for a rescue. A rescue that could turn into a suicide mission if they weren't careful.

Cy broke the silence. "Have we got a com link with the *Claudia*?"

Cap nodded.

"Good," Cy said as he squirted himself toward the comset. "I want a look at their damage reports."

"Captain?" The voice belonged to Rubashkin.

Neubeck felt her head come up, suddenly aware that she'd fallen asleep. A quick glance at the ship's clock confirmed that five minutes had disappeared. Eight hours had passed since the meteor strike and she was very tired.

"Yes?"

"The captain of the *Junk* wants to speak with you."

Neubeck rubbed her eyes. She still couldn't believe it. A tug named *Junk*. She sincerely hoped the name reflected the owner's sense of humor . . . not her actual condition. Well, something was better than nothing, and the other tugs were a long ways off.

Neubeck wanted to know who she was dealing with. "A man or a woman?"

"A man."

"Do we have anything on him?"

Rubashkin had anticipated the captain's question and pushed a button. There were various advantages to working for the Empire Line, and one was a computer loaded with trivial but sometimes useful information. Included were files on all registered ships, their owners, *and* senior officers.

Words appeared on the com screen and Rubashkin waited for her reaction.

Name: Sorenson, Theodore A.
Born: 1-30-3006 Terra
Education: Graduated New Point Prep School 6-17-3023
          Graduated Imperial Maritime Academy 6-24-3028

A surprisingly short list of ships and ranks followed. Neubeck skimmed through them to the final entry:

Assumed command liner *Star of Empire* 3-2-3047
Star of Empire wrecked 11-12-3049
Subject found unfit for duty and relieved of command 8-4-3050.
Presently owner/operator tug *Junk*.

Rubashkin smiled as her eyebrows shot up. "That's right, Captain, he has more than a passing acquaintance with liners in trouble."

Neubeck started to say something but held her tongue instead. Assuming the ship survived she'd face a court of inquiry as well. How would *she* fare? She could almost hear the prosecutor as he or she said, "So, Captain Neubeck, you were asleep when the meteor hit, what happened then?" She pushed the thought aside.

"Put Captain Sorenson on."

The face that appeared on the com screen was long and thin as if suffering from a protracted disease. He had bushy eyebrows, intelligent blue eyes, and a thin-lipped mouth. Neubeck summoned a professional smile.

"Greetings, Captain Sorenson. I look forward to meeting you in person . . . and the sooner the better!"

Cap laughed politely. "I understand. Believe me, the feeling's mutual. And that's why I'm calling. We've got some work to do."

Neubeck sat up a little straighter. Work to do? Great Sol, her people had been working around the clock! She felt defensive and did her best to hide it. "Okay, Captain, what have you got in mind?"

"Not me," Cap answered, "my chief engineer. I'll put him on."

Sorenson disappeared and was replaced by a shot of a floating globe. It extruded a vid pickup and aimed it in her direction. Neubeck glanced at Rubashkin. He smiled and gave a shrug. She managed a straight face.

"Hello, I'm Captain Neubeck."

The globe bobbed up and down. "Glad to meet you, Captain. My name is Cy Borg."

"I'm pleased to meet you," Neubeck replied. "I wish our chief could join in this conversation, but he was killed in the meteor strike."

Cy sank slightly. "Yes, I'm sorry."

Neubeck cleared her throat. "So, what can we do to help?"

Cy was silent for a moment as if gathering his thoughts. "Given your present rate of descent, we'll be lucky to hold you where you are, much less pull you out."

"So?" Neubeck hoped this was going somewhere. She was well acquainted with her ship's situation.

"So," Cy replied, "we'll try to repair drive number two. Number one is a dockyard job, but according to your damage reports, number two remains a possibility. With some power from it, plus what *Junk* can provide, we'll pull you out."

Neubeck shook her head. The cyborg was wasting her time. "Sorry. It's like I said. The chief and all of his officers are dead. Some techs survived but they don't have the knowledge. We even checked the passengers. No luck."

"You don't understand," Cy replied patiently. "*I* have the knowledge, and *I'll* tell your techs what to do."

Neubeck perked up slightly. "You could do that? Direct them from there?"

"Yes, I believe I can," Cy said evenly. "Now here's what I need . . ."

• • •

Durna was a fiery ball that filled most of the main view screen and backlit the liner. Looking at it Lando could almost *feel* the sun trying to pull him down.

From a distance the *Princess Claudia* looked fine. In fact better than "fine." She looked beautiful. In spite of the fact that she would never pass through a planet's atmosphere, her designers had taken care to smooth her skin and make her *look* like what she was. One of the finest ships ever built.

But under high mag Lando could see the point where the meteor had plunged through the liner's outer hull. A rough-and-ready patch had been installed allowing Neubeck to repressurize the drive rooms.

By using jury-rigged vid cams to see what was going on, and by driving the ship's remaining engineering staff to the edge of exhaustion, Cy had accomplished a great deal during *Junk*'s long approach.

But there was still work left to do, dangerous work down inside drive two's reaction chamber, work that they hoped to avoid. There was a chance, a slim one to be sure but a chance, that *Junk* could tow the liner unassisted. Everyone had agreed to give it a try.

Lando used delicate bursts of power to move *Junk* even closer. "You ready, Cap?"

"Ready," Sorenson answered tersely. "Here goes."

There were beads of sweat on Cap's forehead as he reached out with two tractor beams and locked them onto *Claudia*'s hull. "I have lock-on . . . pass the word."

Lando touched a button and Neubeck came on-line. "Captain, we have two-beam lock-on. Applying power now."

Neubeck nodded. "Thank you, Pilot . . . here's hoping it's enough."

Careful to apply the power smoothly Lando brought both of *Junk*'s drives up to max and a little beyond. Twin warning lights and a buzzer came on. He checked the NAVCOMP for a change in position. A yard, a mile, anything. Damn! They were losing ground.

Cy's voice came from *Junk*'s drive room. He'd been monitoring their progress or lack of it.

"It's just as we feared, Pik, she's still falling toward the sun, slower now but falling all the same. Back off the power a bit. Save it for later.

"I'll transfer to the liner in the meantime. Things will go more quickly if I'm there in person, or in housing, as the case may be."

Lando chuckled. "That's a roger. Reducing power now." The buzzer went suddenly silent and the warning lights vanished. He turned toward the com screen.

"Sorry, Captain, it looks like we're going to need drive two."

Neubeck was disappointed but determined to hide it. She forced a smile. "Well, thanks to the hard work by your chief engineer we still have a chance. I'll send my gig."

An indicator light went from green to red. Lando smiled. "Thanks, but that won't be necessary. Engineer Borg is on his way. You might station someone at your main passenger lock though. Cy's in a hurry."

Neubeck frowned, then smiled her understanding. "Of course! The chief has built-in transportation. How convenient."

"It has its moments," Lando agreed. "We'll continue to slow your descent. Let us know when it's time to leave."

Though separated from space by a metal housing Cy came closer than most to direct contact. Because his alloy casing was the same one he lived in all the time there was no sense of putting something between him and the void. He had total freedom to move in any direction that he pleased. It was wonderful, exhilarating, and terrible all at the same time.

The trip from *Junk* to the *Claudia* was one of the loneliest moments of his entire life. There was nothing to be but himself. He felt separate, different, and terribly alone. Suddenly he wanted a body, any body, even one riddled with disease.

He remembered what it was like to be a man. To run, jump, and make love to a woman. He remembered what it was like to make things with his hands. To push, pull, and twist parts together. He remembered what it was like to put everything on one throw of the dice. To lose, cry, and be taken apart.

Where were his arms? His lungs? His heart?

Reaching out to hold someone else's wife? Breathing life

into someone else's dreams? Pumping blood to someone else's brain?

Oh, God! It would be so easy to stop, so easy to turn off the air that pushed him through space, so easy to settle into Durna's warm embrace.

"Cy?" The sound of Melissa's voice jerked him back. There was a multifreq comset built into his electronics. He saw *Claudia*'s lock just ahead.

"Yes?"

"Would they have any ice cream? We're all out."

Cy smiled deep within himself. "Come to think of it, I'll bet they do."

"Could you bring me some?"

The lock opened and Cy squirted himself inside. "Work comes first, but if everything goes well, I'll see what I can do."

"Thanks, Cy! I love you!" and Melissa was gone.

Neubeck sipped her latest cup of black coffee and grimaced at the bitter taste. She was determined to stay on her diet. At least that was something *she* could control.

Neubeck had just completed a tour of the ship and found morale was slipping. The costume ball had been a great success, but there was no hiding the desperate situation, and voices were getting shrill. Rubashkin had been waiting for her return.

"All right, Andre, give me the bad news."

Rubashkin was tired and looked it. His voice sounded slightly hoarse. "We have one, maybe two hours. After that things get ugly. If we wait too long the lifeboats won't have enough power to blast clear. Those little in-system drives weren't designed for this sort of thing."

"We can put some of our passengers aboard the tug."

Rubashkin nodded. "True, but not enough."

"What's the latest on drive two?"

Rubashkin gave a characteristic shrug. "It's down to the wire. Someone's got to enter the reaction chamber and hand align the flux rods. Whoever goes stands a good chance of radiation poisoning."

Neubeck winced. Flux rod alignment was normally carried out by robots. The kind you can find in any good-sized yard but not aboard ship. "Any volunteers?"

"Yeah, the borg's going in."

"The tug's chief engineer?"

"That's right."

"Damn."

"Yeah, damn is right, he's one helluva man."

Neubeck gave it some thought and decided Rubashkin was right. Cy Borg *was* one helluva man. She sipped cold coffee.

"I guess we'd better get everyone onto the boat deck. Load but don't launch."

"Yes, ma'am."

"And, Andre . . ."

"Yes, Captain?"

"If you know any good prayers, say 'em now."

"What's happening now?" Dee was standing behind Lando and looking over his right shoulder while Melissa peeked over his left. The picture quality was extremely poor, and not knowing much about ships, Dee had a hard time understanding what Cy was up to.

"Cy's going in. You see that weird-looking thing they draped over him? Well, that's some makeshift radiation armor. It might protect his brain."

"Might?"

"No one knows. We hope so."

"It will," Melissa said fiercely. "Cy knows what he's doing".

Dee put a hand on Melissa's shoulder and gave a gentle squeeze. "What's the long skinny thing?"

"A flux rod from drive one. One of the rods in drive two is badly bent and Cy's got to replace it. Once that's accomplished he'll make sure the rest of the rods are in alignment, seal the reaction chamber, and restart the drive."

"Yeah," Melissa agreed, "then we have ice cream."

The minutes seemed to crawl by with agonizing slowness as Cy carefully removed the bent flux rod, installed the new one, and began to align the rest. It was a painstaking process full of starts and stops. Finally, after what seemed an eternity, the task was over.

They saw a fuzzy image of Cy leaving the reactor, of it being resealed, of technicians clearing away tools and parts.

Cy disappeared, then reappeared via cleaner video. The awkward shielding was gone, and except for the cable connecting him to a DC power outlet, Cy looked his normal self. He aimed a vid pickup toward the com screen. There was something formal about the way he said it.

"Captain Neubeck, Captain Sorenson, it's now or never."

Neubeck clapped her hands. "Excellent work, Chief! You're incredible!"

Lando looked around. Cap was nowhere in sight. He turned back to the com screen.

"We read you, Cy . . . we're standing by."

It took a good fifteen minutes to bring drive two from zero to fifty percent power. With both ships slipping toward the sun time was of the essence, but so was safety, and the last thing Cy wanted was an accident. If a flux rod was misaligned and they applied power too quickly, the drive could blow up.

But it didn't. Bit by bit the power came up until Neubeck was grinning from ear to ear and Lando was itching to try it.

"Okay," Cy said carefully, "let's give it a whirl. Captain Neubeck . . . ask your pilot to apply power. Gently now . . . let's minimize the stress as much as we can.

"Pik, just keep it steady, and watch those tractor beams. This would be a bad time to lose them."

Pik looked around. Cap was still missing. He had a sudden premonition and punched up the intercom in Cap's cabin. The vid pickup was positioned to cover the desk but he could see the foot of the other man's bunk in the lower right-hand corner of the screen. There was no mistaking Cap's boots.

Damn! Sometime during the last hour or so the worthless bastard had consumed enough booze to pass out. Now he was gone. Out from under the pressure, the tension, and the possibility of failure.

Della and Melissa had taken Cap's place. Melissa knew, Lando could tell from the tight expression on her face, and he felt sorry for her.

As if reading his thoughts Della looked up and smiled. "Don't worry, Pik, we've got it covered, don't we, honey?"

Melissa nodded, and even though she didn't say anything,

Lando thought he saw the trace of a smile. Maybe she'd accept Della after all.

And then, slowly but surely, both ships began to move. Even though they weren't getting more than half power from drive two, it was enough to make the critical difference, and everyone heaved a sigh of relief.

About an hour later they were out of Durna's gravity well and headed for the Imperial navy yard on a planetoid designated as IW-72.

By now the passengers had been sent back to their staterooms to dress for dinner, the other tugs had been sent back home, and Cy had returned to *Junk*.

Neubeck had insisted on sending Cy home in her gig. Lando had to stay on the bridge, but Melissa and Dee were in the tug's launching bay when the hatch opened and Cy floated out.

It was only after the cyborg had received a shower of congratulations and hugs that Melissa noticed the man and woman. They wore identical uniforms and carried a large metal canister between them. The woman smiled. "Don't tell me, let me guess, this is for you."

Melissa's eyes got big. "For me? What is it?"

Cy bobbed up and down. "What do you mean 'what is it?' It's your ice cream."

Melissa grabbed Cy's casing and gave him a big hug. "Thank you, Cy! But it's so big!"

Cy chuckled. "Captain Neubeck does things in a *big* way. Speaking of which I'll bet she'd like her crew back. Now, if you and Della will take the ice cream, these two can return."

Taking the ice cream between them, they thanked the man and woman, and stepped into the lock. As the hatch sealed behind them a sad expression came onto Melissa's face.

Cy saw it and said, "That's a sad expression. What's the matter, hon?"

"I just realized how selfish I am. *You're* the one who fixed everything and *I* got the reward."

Cy wished he could pick her up and hold her but settled for touching her shoulder with a mechanical pincer. "That's not true, Melissa. The truth is that *you* fixed me so *I* could fix them."

Melissa smiled in an automatic sort of way, not understanding, but content to let it go.

But Della looked Cy right in the vid pickup, and although she didn't know exactly what had happened, the softness in her eyes said she cared. Cy felt warm inside. It was something nobody could take away.

16

The inside of the museum was pleasantly cool. It was quiet, like the inside of a church, and refreshing after the hustle and bustle of the streets outside. It was the middle of the week, and outside of a few maintenance bots, Dee had the place to herself. She took a moment to enjoy it.

The museum and the things in it represented a whole universe of knowledge and experience denied Dee due to her childhood. Someday she'd have the time and money to learn. But not now. Now there were other things to do.

The better part of a week had passed since they had delivered the *Princess Claudia* to the Imperial navy yard on IW-72 and made their way to Pylax.

After refueling *Junk* and performing some much-needed maintenance, the crew went dirtside for a hero's welcome. Everyone except Lando, who remained behind to keep an eye on the ship and avoid bounty hunters.

Dee looked around the cavernous lobby and wondered if Lando liked museums. Somehow she thought he would. This one had high-vaulted ceilings. There was no ornamentation, no fixtures, nothing.

The chem-painted walls produced a soft white light that seemed to come from everywhere at the same time. It oozed from ceiling and walls to balance itself out and erase shadows. In this museum every painting, every sculpture, would receive equal treatment, and leave nothing in dark corners.

Dee's boots made a clacking sound on the marbled floor as she approached the floating sculpture. Although it *seemed* real, the art was purely electronic, and would vanish at the touch of a button.

Manifesting itself as a silver ball the electro-sculpture was pierced here and there by irregular holes. Dee looked through them and saw herself peering back.

She looked around for the vid cams that must be there but couldn't see them.

The sculpture reminded her of Cy. Thanks to unending praise from Captain Neubeck and his status as a cyborg, the engineer had been the very center of all the press attention. The near calamity was a big story and was making its way through the empire just as fast as the newscorp message torps could carry it.

So Cy was a hero, a situation that he found to be more than a little amusing, and tended to play down. But modest or not there was no escaping the press and at this very moment the engineer was attending a luncheon in his honor.

Cap would be there too, along with Melissa, and together the three of them would receive a really huge salvage check from the Empire Line. All had expected a lengthy wait before seeing the money. But thanks to the press attention and Captain Neubeck's urging, the company had settled right away.

It was not Dee's kind of affair, and thanks to her secondary role, she'd been able to beg off. And since she couldn't return to *Junk* until the others were done, the art museum made a wonderful sanctuary.

Dee had always enjoyed sculpture, especially the kind you could see with your hands as well as your eyes, and was soon lost in a room full of abstract shapes.

The sculptures came in a wonderful variety of materials, ranging from native stone, to wood, to metal and fused glass. Many were imbued with mechanical motion, or stood on rotating platforms, twirling for her inspection.

Maybe that's why she missed the gleam of light on chrome, the surreptitious movement, and the faint whine of servos.

Whatever the reason Dee was completely unprepared when Jord Willer stepped out from between two sculptures and pointed the automatic shotgun her way.

She turned and looked for a way out but found there were two people behind her. One was a hard-looking woman dressed in slug-proof monster skins from the planet Swamp. Her body seemed to shimmer as the skins tried to match the background. At times it looked as though her head was floating in midair.

But there was no mistaking the blaster or the skillful way she held it.

Her companion was different. A tall, slender man in a black frock coat. He was armed but with what? There was no way to tell. The man had hooded hawk eyes, a predatory nose, and a smile that held little humor.

Turning back toward the cyborg Dee prepared to die. After all she'd blinded Willer's ship and humiliated him. It was part of her profession, part of the unwritten code, kill or be killed.

Dee had lived with the code for years now and felt little more than a sense of mild regret. She'd never know where things might have gone with Lando, never know if another life was possible, never know what could've been.

Then those thoughts were gone, replaced by a computerlike analysis of movements and trajectories. Yes, there were three of them, enough to kill her, but they'd pay a price. One, maybe two, would die with her. The first would be Willer.

"Ah yes," Willer said sarcastically. "The bounty hunter figures the odds, and prepares to take someone with her. Me perhaps? Yes, of course. But wait . . . perhaps she should think . . . consider the fact that my finger is already on the trigger. Better yet, maybe she should listen, and see if death is the only choice."

Dee felt her heartbeat slow just a hair. The borg wanted to talk, some sort of a deal perhaps, more time in any case. She forced a grin.

"It seems you have my full attention. What's on your mind?"

The shotgun dropped a little but still pointed in her general direction. Willer smiled. "Don't get the wrong idea, I *do* want to kill you, but I want something else even more."

"The *Star of Empire.*"

"You're very perceptive. If it still exists, I want the *Star of Empire* just as much as Sorenson does, but for different reasons. What *he* lost was a reputation he didn't deserve, and a job he hadn't done for years.

"What I lost was a good deal more. I lost my body, my center of being, my image of myself.

"Do you know what that's like? To lose the picture you have of yourself?" Willer shook his head.

"No, of course you don't. It's something only cyborgs understand.

"Well, Sorenson took it from me. He took my life, my future, and my dreams. So I want the *Star*. I want her for the money, for the pleasure of having her, and to keep her out of Sorenson's drunken hands."

Willer stared into Dee's eyes as if trying to impress his thoughts on her by force of will. "I'll tell you something, bounty hunter, something I've never shared with another living soul. I'm convinced that somehow, some way, Sorenson *knows* where the *Star* is located. Weird, huh? But I *feel* it and know it's true."

Dee swallowed hard. On the one hand it seemed as if Willer was more than a few planets short of a full system. On the other hand there was the matter of Sorenson's coordinates. What if they were real? She played along.

"So? Where do I come in?"

"You have an opportunity," Willer answered softly. "An opportunity to live and profit in the process. Thanks to the salvage Sorenson has more money than ever before. He'll use it to resume the search. Soon, within days, he'll head for the asteroid belt. You'll go with him. My crew and I will follow. Then, when the critical moment arrives, you'll strike from within."

Dee considered the cyborg's proposal. What he wanted her to do was no worse than many things she'd done in the past. Still, the thought of Lando, of Melissa, even of Cap hardened her resolve. She would not betray her friends.

Fine, but should she lie? Tell him what he wanted to hear? Buy time? No, something about him, something about his expression, demanded the truth. Dee got ready to pull her gun. She gestured with her left hand to pull his attention away from her right.

"Thanks, but no thanks, I'll take my chances right here."

Time stretched thin. Dee waited for the cyborg to move, waited for the slug between the shoulder blades, waited to give and receive death. It never came. Willer allowed the barrel of his shotgun to fall toward the floor.

"You gave the correct answer, bounty hunter. I place no value on words said under duress. But I believe in *you*. I believe in your hunger, your need for more, your predatory instincts.

"So I make you this offer: When the time comes, take my part, and I'll give you ten percent of whatever's realized.

"Right now you say no, but during the coming days you'll think about it, dream about it, and want it. In the end you'll make the right decision."

Dee looked over her shoulder at the man and woman, then back to Willer. "Am I free to go?"

Light rippled off the cyborg's upper torso. For one brief moment he looked like one of the sculptures that surrounded him. Then he spoke. "No, Dee, there's one more thing."

Strong arms grabbed Dee from behind. She struggled but it was too late. The man and woman had her.

Willer approached until his Adonis-like features were only a foot away. His words came out like the hiss of a snake. "Even though I desire your cooperation I cannot allow your actions to go unpunished."

He gave a twisted smile. "It would set a bad example for the others."

The cyborg held up a hand. There in his huge palm Dee saw a small disk. It was secured to his middle finger by a ring.

"You know what this is?"

Dee felt something heavy fall into her gut. "A neuro-stim."

"That's right. A little reminder of what happens to those who cross me."

Willer placed both hands on either side of her head much like a parent preparing to kiss a small child. Dee felt the disk free itself from the ring and bond to her skin.

Willer stepped back. "Until we meet again."

The pain came like a white-hot spear. It filled her brain with fire and ran like molten metal through every nerve. Her body jerked and spasmed. She staggered around in circles, bumped into a large sculpture, and sent it crashing to the floor. With darkness came relief.

When Dee awoke it was to the feeling of movement and cold stone under her cheek. Something had her by one foot and was dragging her across the floor.

Sitting up she saw that a medium-sized maintenance bot had spotted her, taken her for a drunk, and was dragging her toward the door.

"Hey! Stop that! Let go!"

The sound of her voice made Dee's head throb but had the desired effect. The maintenance bot dropped her foot and whirred away. A couple of other robots were struggling to right a fallen statue. There was no sign of Willer or his crew.

Dee ached all over. She checked for injuries. There were none as far as she could tell. Neuro-stims were incredibly painful but left no bone or tissue damage. Unless you broke something while thrashing around, that is.

Dee felt dizzy. It took a while to stand up. Finally she made it. Staggering past the sculptures, past the electro-sculpture, she made it to the door. It slid aside.

Outside it was bright and sunny. The warmth felt good on Dee's face.

The tender had been back for an hour now. Cy was puttering around the drive room, Melissa was tucked into bed, and Cap had passed out. It was amazing that he could even walk much less fly the tender.

There was a tap on the door frame. Lando didn't turn. He continued to stuff clothes into a duffel bag. "Yes?"

"I wondered where you were."

Dee's voice was level but he sensed the tension. He knew what she really meant but refused to acknowledge it. How could he? How could he do anything with a price on his head?

"Just gathering up some odds and ends. It's amazing how much baggage you can collect in a short period of time."

Dee lounged in his doorway. "Yes, and how easily you can leave it all behind."

Lando turned. "That's not fair, Della. I don't want to run. But I haven't got much choice. I've got some money now, enough to get a long ways away, far enough to start over."

Her red hair shimmered as Della shook her head. "It won't work, Pik. I found you, and others will too. There's thousands of bounty hunters out there. How many can you kill before they kill you? Very few will give up a rich bounty for your questionable charms."

There, it was out in the open, for better or worse. There was a long silence as each searched the other's eyes. It was a turning point, a critical moment in both lives, and each of them knew it.

Dee had considered telling Lando about Willer, about the neuro-stim, but decided to wait. It was something he needed to know, but not here, not now.

Now she wanted a decision based on emotions other than anger at what Willer had done to her, and fear of what he might do to Cap and Melissa.

Lando spoke first. "I wondered if you'd come with me . . . but didn't dare ask. I don't have much to offer."

Dee smiled softly. "You have yourself. You're worth money. That's more than most men can say."

Lando laughed. "All right then, come with me! We'll find something out along the rim, a little freight line maybe, or a farm."

Dee shook her head. "It won't work, Pik, not until you get the price off your head."

"So what's the alternative?"

"Stay aboard, save your money, hire a good lawyer."

"And in the meantime?"

"And in the meantime we'll see. Good things take time."

Lando walked over to the hatch. Dee stepped into his arms.

"How much time?"

"As much as it takes."

"You're beautiful, but frustrating."

She smiled. "I'm glad you noticed."

Dee started to say something else but Lando's lips covered hers and the words were forever lost.

17

With every sensor on max, and Lando's nerves stretched tight, *Junk* approached Gate Twenty-one. If he'd learned anything during his first trip to Durna's asteroid belt, Lando had learned that gates were dangerous as hell. First there were the pirates, and then there was Willer, either one of whom could be waiting in ambush.

Lando was furious over the cyborg's attack on Dee and only her stubborn resistance had kept him from tracking Willer down.

Dee wanted revenge too, but said it was stupid to attack someone on their ground, and smart to wait for a better opportunity. Lando had reluctantly agreed.

But forewarned is forearmed and after leaving Pylax, Lando detected a tail. The other vessel was too far away for positive identification but there was little doubt as to the ship's identity. Willer was following them. He knew where *Junk* was headed and intended to share in anything the tug found.

Lando responded with a trick learned from his smuggler father. Although hyperspace jumps are normally reserved for long distances, they can be used in-system, and a series of quick hops is almost impossible to follow. And because they are carefully calculated within a volume of known space, they're reasonably safe.

So Lando set up the NAVCOMP, turned it loose, and tried to keep his lunch down while *Junk* made a series of stutter jumps. His stomach never had approved of hyperspace jumps and six in a row was about five too many.

The crew meanwhile was on full alert. Cap had strapped himself into the top weapons turret with Cy to starboard and Dee to port. The addition of Dee to *Junk*'s crew had strengthened their defensive capabilities considerably.

Lando checked his sensors one last time. Nothing.

"See anything?"

The voice belonged to Cap. The combination of tension and an ugly hangover had coarsened his voice.

"Nothing so far," Lando answered. "Nothing but a zillion asteroids, any one of which could hide a pirate ship."

"Or *be* a pirate ship," Melissa said, remembering their last run-in with the roid pirates.

"I heard they nailed that bunch some weeks back," Cy put in. "The leader was a Finthian."

"I hope you're right," Lando said tersely. " 'Cause here we go!"

It was impossible to put on much speed without running the risk of a collision, but Lando crossed his fingers and punched up fifty percent power.

A few seconds later they were inside the belt and working their way through the maze of slowly tumbling rock. There was no attack. The crew let out a collective sigh of relief.

Lando tapped some keys and watched Cap's coordinates appear on the nav screen. A roid miner's lie? A way to turn a fast credit? Or Sol's own truth?

There was, as Cap put it, "only one way to find out."

It wouldn't be easy. Lando made a face at the screen. In order to reach those coordinates he'd have to pick his way through the worst part of the belt. The part that was only superficially charted, the part where the asteroids were thicker than Ip Mites on a Zerk Monkey's tail, the part where smart people didn't go.

"Well, that explains why I'm here," Lando mumbled to himself, and began the long torturous process of finding his way through the belt.

It took the better part of two standard days to reach the correct quadrant and ease their way in toward the point specified by the coordinates. Long hard days of unrelenting concentration, tension, and hard work.

The asteroids were thick, so thick that most showed signs of multiple collisions, a fact that didn't bode well for their mission. After all, if the asteroids bumped into each other that frequently, how 'bout a ship? Wouldn't it be hit as well? And a single collision would destroy even the largest vessel.

Cy put the odds of finding the ship at just about zero and Lando agreed. That's why he came a half foot out of his chair when the alarms went off.

The sensors thought they'd located another ship but that couldn't be! For one thing they were still a half day out from the roid miner's coordinates, and for another the readouts didn't make sense.

Lando scanned the board. What the hell was going on? The sensors claimed there was metal up ahead, lots of it, and a substantial amount of heat as well. But how could that be?

"What've you got?" Lando turned to find Cap at his shoulder. The other man had whiskey breath, shiny skin, and unnaturally bright eyes.

"I'm not sure, Cap. Something that's made of metal and generates lots of heat."

Cap's face dropped. "Generates heat?" Like Lando, Cap knew that the liner's drives would be stone-cold. That left two possibilities. Some sort of mining rig or a pirate.

Cap turned away. "I'll man my weapon."

Lando nodded. "An excellent idea." He punched the intercom. "Battle stations, everybody . . . there's something strange up ahead. All weapons are armed."

"That's a roger," Dee answered. "The port blister is on-line and ready to go."

"Ditto the starboard," Cy answered.

"The top turret is on-line," Cap added tensely. "Tell us what you see."

Lando didn't bother to answer. He was too busy sliding around a rather large asteroid. Lando kept it between *Junk* and the metallic object for as long as he could. But the moment finally came when he couldn't hide any longer and the tug was forced out into the open.

Lando couldn't believe his eyes! Beyond the asteroid there was an open space, and in the middle of the open space there was a ship! A long, thick ovoid and, as far as Lando could tell, largely undamaged.

That was strange enough, but the vessel also gave off a greenish glow as if lit from within, and was flooding his sensors with interference.

Lando touched a button and shunted video to the top weapons turret. "We've got something, Cap. Is that the *Star of Empire*?"

There was a moment of silence as Cap studied the video, then a long drawn-out sigh. Lando could almost hear the hope flowing out of him.

But to Cap's credit he kept his composure. "Nope, I don't know what that is, but it's not the *Star*. That greenish glow is very strange. Try for a contact."

Lando turned to the com screen. "Unknown vessel, this is the salvage vessel *Junk,* do you read me?"

The response was sudden and completely unexpected. Dee saw it coming, tried to give warning, but couldn't speak the words fast enough. "Watch out, Pik . . . it launched some sort of . . ."

Then Lando saw it for himself. A green blob that raced toward them and hit the ship's hull.

Much to Lando's surprise the blob passed right through *Junk*'s protective force field without setting off a single alarm. A hallucination? No, it hit *Junk* with enough force to rock the entire ship and snap his head back.

Suddenly every one of Lando's screens were filled with snow and his instruments produced impossible readings.

Parallel lines of blue light stuttered out toward the other ship as Cap fired his weapon. His voice was tinged with panic. "Fire! Fire! Fire!"

Lando cut power to Cap's weapons turret with the flip of a switch. "Hold it, Cap. This thing's weird, but not necessarily hostile."

The control room was suddenly full of greenish light. "What the hell?"

The external vid cams were flickering on and off but Lando could still see enough to understand what was going on. The blob was directly overhead and sliding the length of *Junk*'s hull. As it moved, the greenish light moved with it, and passed through solid durasteel as if it weren't even there. Two seconds later and it was gone.

"Very interesting," Cy said calmly. "I don't know about the rest of the ship, but at present the drive room is full of greenish light. I have the feeling we're being scanned."

The engineer's calm appraisal helped Lando understand what his eyes had already seen. "I think Cy's right, and not only that, but did you see those energy beams? They didn't even scratch that ship! It's as if they were neutralized somehow."

"Or simply absorbed," Cy added calmly. "The green light just disappeared."

"Look! The bloblike thing is connected to some sort of tether!" The voice was Dee's.

Lando looked and sure enough, the protoplasm was connected to some sort of a long green tether, which was pulling it toward the ship. He noticed that as the blob moved farther away his instruments began to clear.

Lando flipped the center bow cam to high mag and scanned the other ship's hull. He gave the others a running narration of what he saw.

"I'm using high mag. I see a weird hull. There's no surface installations like you'd see on one of our ships. Lots of blobs though, each fastened to the ship with a green tether, and all of 'em green."

"Still no contact?" Cap inquired, his voice a bit shaky.

Dee gave a snort of derision. "Still no contact? Come on, Cap, you've gotta be kidding! Lando gives 'em a call and they send a green blob to ram your ship? How much contact do you want?"

"I think Dee's right," Cy said thoughtfully. "The blob was a response to Pik's attempt at communication. Now it's waiting to see what we'll do next."

"It? Why 'it'? Why not 'them'?" The question was Dee's but Lando wondered too.

"Maybe it *is* 'them,'" the cyborg responded, "but I don't think so. That's a very advanced construct. It has already demonstrated a level of technological sophistication beyond anything I've ever seen or heard of. If the owners were aboard they'd be telling us what to do . . . or simply swatting us like flies."

"Maybe," Dee said doubtfully. "That's what *we'd* do. But *they* might react in a completely different manner."

There was a long period of silence while everyone took it in. Cy was at least partially right. Regardless of whether the owners were aboard or not, the ship represented an unheard of level of scientific achievement, and that could have implications for the entire human race.

That was their first thought. Their second was less altruistic. Given that the drifter was loaded with advanced technology, and given that the owners might be somewhere else, what was the ship worth?

"I'm going aboard." The voice belonged to Cy and carried so much conviction that no one even thought to argue with him.

"Me too." Sorenson's voice seemed to gain strength as he spoke.

"First we'll find out if anyone's aboard, then assuming they aren't, we'll take control of the ship. I'll take a look at the controls while Cy checks the power plant. Just think! That power plant's been running for who knows how long! Maybe hundreds of years!"

"Maybe thousands," Cy added, but Cap ignored him.

"Whatever. The main thing is to take control, establish full salvage rights, and get the ship out of here in one piece."

"I want to go too," Melissa said. "Can I, Daddy? Can I please?"

"No you can't," Cap replied sternly. "You'll stay here. Watch her, Lando, and depressurize the bay. Who knows what kind of atmosphere we'll find aboard that ship. I'll suit-up and meet Cy at the tender."

There was an angry click as Melissa dropped off the intercom. Lando was sympathetic, but knew Cap was right, and in her heart of hearts Melissa knew it too. He touched a button. "Hey, Della."

"Yeah?"

"Take Cap's position in the top turret. I'll delegate sensor control to you. Ignore the drifter and keep your eyes peeled for bad guys. What with the tender outside, and a major tow to deal with, our buns are hanging in the breeze."

"Speak for yourself," Dee replied primly. "My buns are right where they belong. Besides, the only breeze around here comes off the intercom."

Lando grinned and leaned back in his chair. His eyes went to the alien drifter. The halo of greenish light seemed to fluctuate slightly, as though the ship were alive, and breathing ever so slightly.

The alien ship filled Cy with a sense of wonder. As they came closer it filled the tender's view screens with luminescent light. Strangely enough the electronic interference they'd experienced farther out had largely disappeared. The drifter was long, longer than the *Star of Empire* had been, and twice as big around.

The big green blobs clung to its hull like fungi feeding on a dead log. Every now and then one would suddenly expand and soar outward trailing a tendril of greenish light. Meanwhile others returned and took their places along the ship's outer surface.

At first Cy assumed the greenish tethers were used to reel the blobs in, but then he realized he was wrong, and that the tendrils became shorter. It seemed as though the connective stuff was reabsorbed into the ship's hull when it wasn't needed.

Plastic hull material? Some sort of new force field? The possibilities made Cy's brain spin.

For his part Cap was less concerned about the how and why of the drifter's operation and more occupied with the pragmatics of taking possession. The rest could wait till later.

Sorenson licked dry lips. God what he wouldn't give for a drink right now. He usually kept a bottle stashed inside the first-aid kit but someone had found and removed it. Melissa probably. Never mind, the bottle was gone, and he'd have to get along without it.

The first problem was already behind them. For better or worse the drifter and/or its occupants had allowed them to approach. Sorenson had half expected to die, but not seeing a way around it, he had forced himself to take the chance. Now they were only a thousand feet away and still alive.

Okay, time to tackle the second problem, getting aboard. Cap put the tender into a tight turn and slid down the vessel's port side.

Well, he assumed it was the port side, but come to think of it there was no way to tell bow from stern. Maybe its owners didn't think in terms of "front" and "back," maybe they went everywhere sideways, or who knows? But surely they had a way to enter and leave the ship.

They completed another entire length of the ship without sign of a hatch or other opening. Cap made another tight turn. It had to be there.

"Keep your pickups peeled, Cy, we need a way to get aboard."

Cy was silent for a moment. "Try telling *it* that." He'd debated whether to say "them" or "it" and settled on the latter. Cy wasn't sure why, but the engineer in him felt they were dealing with complicated machinery rather than sentient minds.

Cap gave him a "what the hell are you thinking" look, but stabbed a button and spoke into the comset anyway. "This is Captain Sorenson of the vessel *Junk,* requesting permission to come aboard."

The response was immediate and frightening. One of the green blobs burst up from the drifter's hull to enclose the tender and pull it down. Cap started to apply more power but Cy stopped him.

"Hold it, Cap! You asked for permission to come aboard, and that's what you got!"

Cap put the drive on standby and forced his hands away from the controls. Cy was right. Somehow the alien ship had understood and obeyed him.

Greenish light flooded the cabin. Cap looked at Cy. "What is it? Some sort of telepathy?"

Cy spun left and right as if shaking his head. "No, not in the normal sense anyhow, because the only time it reacts is when you use the comset. Unless you put your words into electronic form it can't understand."

Cap looked at the now blank view screens and shook his head in amazement. "Really? But how could it understand Terran?"

Cy bobbed slightly. "Beats me. Let's try something else. Pik will be worried. Tell him we're okay."

Cap touched a button and spoke into the comset. "Tender to *Junk,* don't worry, Lando, we're okay. You read me?"

Nothing but static.

Cy squirted himself forward. "The blob is blocking our signal. Now ask it to relay our signal and see what happens."

Cap activated the comset. "This is Captain Sorenson. Please relay the following signal to my ship. Tender to *Junk,* can you read me, Lando?"

Lando's voice boomed in over the comset. "Loud and clear, Cap . . . you gave us quite a scare. What the hell's going on?"

Cap was just coming to the end of his explanation when the blob disappeared. Cy was the first to notice. "Look, Cap! We're inside the ship!"

Cap looked up at the view screens and saw Cy was correct. The tender had come to rest in a large open area. There were things around them but only dimly seen.

"You still read me, Lando?"

"Crystal clear."

"Good. The blob thing pulled us inside the ship."

"How? We didn't see a hatch or anything."

"I don't know," Cap answered, "but we're here."

He glanced at the board. "Believe it or not my instruments show a breathable atmosphere. I'm going out for a look around."

"Be careful, Daddy!"

Sorenson felt a lump form in his throat. "Don't worry, Mel . . . I'll wear my suit just in case. I'll talk to you in a little bit."

Lando sat up straight. "Did you see that?"

"I sure did," Dee replied emphatically. "The drifter used one of those green blobs to move an asteroid."

"Well, to fend one off anyway," Lando suggested. "I'll bet it pushes them away on a regular basis. That's how it made the big open space."

"Sure," Dee agreed. "Now we know *how*. The question is *why*."

The rain made a drumming noise on Cy's metal casing. Good thing he was waterproof. The rain, like the strange foliage to either side, seemed to confirm a complete self-maintaining biosphere.

Unlike humans and many other aliens, the drifter's architects preferred a natural environment. Natural for *them* that is. The lighter-than-Terran gravity, alien plants, and slightly humid air seemed strange to Cy.

The cyborg had traveled quite a ways by now. He'd seen deserts, grasslands, and even a miniature forest of double-trunked trees. Trees that seemed to have special significance.

Here and there, tucked away among the trees, Cy found dozens of nest beds. That's what he called them anyway and the name seemed to fit. They were depressions really, long indentations in the ground that were padded with spongy stuff and covered with brightly colored blankets.

What were they? Crew quarters? That's the way it seemed but Cy couldn't be sure.

There were plenty of paths, narrow winding affairs mostly, which served as highways for a variety of small animals. There were birds too, and small insects, but no sign of sentient beings.

Missing was any sign of the pipes, duct work, electric conduit, fiber optic cable, and other installations that characterized the interior of most ships.

At one point Cy had paused to scrape the mosslike growth from the inside of the hull. After extruding a sophisticated electrode, he found the hull material was not only conductive, but heavily laden with all sorts of electronic activity.

Somewhere aboard ship an extremely sophisticated artificial intelligence was using the hull to route electronic signals throughout the vessel. He couldn't prove it but thought power was distributed the same way.

Thanks to the special hull material the aliens had been able to dispense with the need for wire, cable, and conduit. It was wonderful, incredible, and absolutely beautiful.

In fact the more Cy saw, the more he knew the ship was a technological treasure trove, a turning point for any society that owned it. Assuming they could bring the ship out of the belt he and his crew mates would never have to work again.

Why then did he feel a hollowness in his nonexistent gut? A growing fear that things wouldn't be that simple? He pushed the feeling aside.

The biosphere came to an end and funneled itself into a sizable lock. From the high overhead and location of various fittings Cy deduced that its designers were most likely tall and skinny.

The ship seemed to sense Cy's presence and know exactly what to do. The lock cycled closed, then open. Cy came out to find himself floating in the middle of an engineer's dream.

Here were the technological underpinnings of everything he'd seen so far. Here were power plants that never broke down. Here were racks full of mysterious components, lights that signified things unknown, and a control area like none he'd seen before.

It consisted of ten black globes. Each globe sat on a white pedestal and helped make a perfect circle. From the chairs located directly in front of the globes Cy deduced they were positions of some kind.

Squirting himself over to the nearest position Cy extended a cautious pincer. Much to his surprise it went right through the globe's seemingly solid surface.

There was a brief moment of disorientation followed by the knowledge that he was somewhere else. Somewhere inside a bio-control system, sampling the ship's atmosphere, and balancing evaporation against rainfall.

Cy jerked his pincer back and the sensation was gone. Holy Sol! What a ship! You could climb inside the controls!

Cy raced to the next black globe, and the next, finding and identifying controls for the power plants, the green blobs, and the ship itself. Lando would love it! A ship he could fly from the inside out! Assuming they could figure things out, of course. Cy went to work.

Since Cy had turned right, toward what Cap thought of as the ship's stern, he went left. Most of the ships he'd seen, human and alien alike, put the control section toward the bow. So, why not this one?

Besides, the launching bay was huge, and full of interesting shapes. What would he find? Valuable cargo? An alien shuttle? Cap set off to find out.

It was dark in the bay, but true to his word Cap was wearing his suit, so he turned on the helmet light. It threw an elongated circle of light up ahead and moved when he did. At first it skittered across faintly phosphorescent hull material but then it touched something shiny.

Cap turned his head left in order to aim the light. What he saw made him gasp with surprise. It was an unmanned probe, an old one, pre-Confederation if he was any judge.

Stepping up for a closer look Cap saw a nameplate. It read "Voyager 2" in Terran script. Damn! He'd have to look it up to be sure, but chances were that thing was more than a thousand years old.

Cap moved on. The air that came in through his open visor

was wet and heavy. He saw a lump up ahead. Turning his head he placed the circle of light right on it. What the hell? Part of a small spaceship. The stern from the look of it. The metal was too torn and twisted to make out more than that.

The light moved back and forth. Wait a minute, what was that? Something shiny, something round, a satellite! Or was it? He'd never seen one exactly like it. Alien probably.

And there, wasn't that a message torp? Yes it was. Later he'd open it up and see what was inside. You never know, it could be something valuable.

And so it went. During the next half hour Cap found fuel tanks, a six-armed space suit with something dead inside, pieces of twisted metal, alien constructs he couldn't name, and a lot more.

It was as if the ship, or its owners, had a propensity for collecting junk. Not for any special purpose, but just for the heck of it. Fascinating stuff but something to investigate later.

Cap was just about to break it off and go looking for the control room when he saw something familiar up ahead. Familiar, but not so familiar that he knew what it was.

His light bounced over metal and slid across the deck. Tilting his head up Cap saw it. A lifeboat. A beat-up lifeboat with a cracked canopy, dented hull, and the name *Star of Empire* stenciled across its bow.

Cap began to scream.

18

It took the better part of two days to prepare the tow. Although Cy's investigations indicated that the drifter might be able to proceed under its own power, there was too much they didn't know about the ship's operation, so a tow seemed like the best way to go.

No simple matter in open space and considerably more difficult in the crowded confines of the asteroid belt.

In order to assure maneuverability it was necessary to mount heavy-duty auxiliary thrusters on the outer surface of the drifter's hull. The thrusters, and the fuel tanks that supplied them, were cumbersome and hard to work with. Even in zero G they had to be guided into place, secured to the hull, and test fired.

Added to that was the fact that they were shorthanded due to Cap's encounter with the lifeboat. Seeing the boat and the name across the bow had pushed Sorenson into a state of hysteria.

Hearing Sorenson's screams via suit radio Cy had responded as quickly as he could. A sedative, followed by enforced rest aboard the tender, had helped a lot. Though shaky Cap was starting to recover.

In the meantime Lando and Dee had been forced to perform almost all of the work associated with placing the thrusters and preparing both ships for the tow.

Back aboard *Junk*, and still sweaty from the hours spent in his suit, Lando ran a final check on the auxiliary thrusters. Dee assisted while Melissa kept watch in the tug's top turret.

By mutual agreement, Lando, Cy, and Dee had kept her in the dark regarding Cap's condition. After all, there was nothing she could do other than worry, so why put her through it?

Lando tapped some keys on a jury-rigged auxiliary control board. Miles away a thruster fired in response. It shut down a fraction of a second later.

"Bow thruster, port side."

Dee looked at the portacomp sitting on her lap. "Check."

"Bow thruster, starboard side."

"Check."

"Midship thruster, port side."

"Check."

"Midship thruster, starboard side."

"Hold . . . I show a control anomaly."

Keys clicked under Lando's fingers. The computer ran a diagnostic routine on the starboard side, midship thruster and sent the results to Dee.

"Anomaly resolved. Control green."

Lando nodded. "Good. Stern thruster, port side."

"Check."

Melissa interrupted. Her voice was a high-pitched squeak. "Pik . . . Della . . . I've got something on the sensors! Something besides the drifter I mean. It's big and headed this way!"

Lando swore softly. Of all times why now? He turned toward Dee. She was gone. The bounty hunter would relieve Melissa and assign her to a less critical weapon.

Lando spoke into the comset and activated *Junk*'s weapons at the same time.

"Cy? Listen, we've got company. No ID . . . but pirates seem like a good possibility. Have you found any weapons on that tub?"

In between nursing Cap, and doing what he could to assist the others, Cy had been deciphering the ship's systems. He had lots left to learn but had a fairly good idea of what the ship could and couldn't do. None of the ten black globes corresponded to weapons systems so he assumed there were none.

"No weapons, Pik . . . at least none so far. It seems our friends are, or were, peace-loving citizens."

"No wonder they aren't around," Lando said cynically.

"Well, seal her up as best you can. It's too late to retrieve the tender. Besides, from what we saw earlier, that baby can take lots of punishment. You're safer where you are."

Cy was just about to point out that personal safety was not his number one goal when another voice cut him off.

"Well, well. Look what we have here. It isn't the *Star of Empire,* but it looks like Captain Sorenson found himself a ship, an alien ship at that."

The audio was being piped over the intercom so Dee and Melissa heard it too.

Dee said, "Uh-oh, we're in trouble now."

And Melissa said, "Don't let him bully you, Pik! Show him who's boss!"

Lando sighed. He should've known. Jord Willer. *Hercules* was still a long ways off but quite recognizable under high mag. He fired all the weapons delegated to automatic and hoped for a lucky hit. Who knows, maybe Willer had left his force field down.

No such luck. All of *Junk*'s energy beams and missiles exploded harmlessly as they hit the other ship's protective field.

Willer returned fire. Because the other vessel was still a ways off *Junk* was able to shrug it off but Lando was worried. *Hercules* was larger and, in spite of *Junk*'s considerable weaponry, even more heavily armed. It might take a while, but in an all-out battle the other ship would win. The bombardment stopped as suddenly as it began.

Willer's perfect face appeared on the com screen. The cyborg's placid features were at odds with his words.

"You're going to pay for that, Lando. You, and Sorenson, and his daughter, and the bounty hunter. All of you will die. As for the borg, well, he can live. Professional courtesy you know. Never kill a fellow freak."

Lando decided to stall. Maybe something would break his way.

"I love you too. But don't count your corpses till you kill them. The drifter's loaded with weapons. Come any closer and we'll turn your ship into scrap metal."

Willer grinned stiffly. "Give me a break, Lando. I heard the borg tell you it was harmless. Stalling is a waste of time. Save me the trouble. Shoot yourself now."

Lando forced a smile. "Hey, you can't blame a guy for trying. How did you find us anyhow?"

Willer shook his head sadly. "Still stalling. Still wasting my time. Well, why not? I'm proud of it actually. The bounty hunter led us here."

For one brief moment Lando wondered if Della had sold them out. But he knew the answer was no. Her words confirmed it.

"You followed me? Why you lying pile of chrome-plated crap! I didn't tell you a thing!"

Willer laughed. "Not directly, my dear, but tell me you did. The confrontation in the museum was staged for your benefit. It provided an excuse to put you out and hide a specially designed beacon inside your body. It was a quick little operation and after the neuro-stim you didn't even notice the pain. Next time you take a shower look for a tiny incision covered with plastiflesh.

"By the way, both of my assistants had some nice things to say about your breasts. Unfortunately my interest disappeared along with my balls."

Dee opened up with her energy cannon but it made little difference. The force field around *Hercules* seemed to expand and contract along with Willer's laughter.

Sorenson's breath came in ragged gasps and his hands shook as he powered up. First the lifeboat, now Willer. He'd heard the whole thing over the tender's comset. Why couldn't they just leave him alone?

Cap's hands shook as they moved over the controls. Power up, repellers on, support systems in the green. He touched a button.

"This is Captain Sorenson requesting permission to leave your launching bay."

This time Cap was ready when a green blob enfolded the tender and lifted it upward.

"Cap? Cap, this is Lando. What the hell are you doing? Stay where you are. I repeat, *stay* where you are."

There was no reply. Lando watched a green blob erupt from the port side of drifter's hull, drift upward, and pop like an overfilled balloon. The tender appeared as if by magic. It turned and headed away from *Junk*.

Lando stabbed a button on the comset. "Cap . . . where the hell are you going?"

Willer appeared on the com screen. He gave a throaty chuckle. "He's running away. That's what he does best. The only surprise is that he's sober enough to fly a ship."

The next voice was Melissa's. "Daddy! Tell them it isn't true! You're not running away, are you?"

Silence.

"Damn you, Daddy! Damn you to hell!" Bright blue energy reached out to touch the tender but missed.

Lando killed power to her weapon. "Stop it, Melissa! That won't solve a thing."

All he heard was a sob and a click as she dropped off the line. Willer attacked a fraction of a second later. Lando responded with everything *Junk* had.

Energy beams lashed out to link the ships together with a pattern of stuttering blue light. Missiles raced from launchers, torpedoes accelerated toward their targets, and force fields flashed incandescent as they struggled to protect their respective vessels.

Lando watched his instruments. Before long *Junk*'s defenses would start to crumble. When they did he'd call the others to the bridge. At least they'd be together.

Cy was angry, damned angry, and determined to do something about it. How dare that chrome-plated space head call him a freak! And try to kill his friends! Well, he'd show Willer a thing or two.

Cy hovered in front of a black globe. His pincer slid through its shiny surface. Suddenly Cy was at the center of a complicated organism. He had hundreds of hands and arms each waiting to do his bidding. The cyborg found that he could see in a 360-degree circle, and hear along the entire range of radio frequencies.

Light flared and static rumbled as two ships hurled death at each other. One was larger and he could see its weapons taking a steady toll. The smaller vessel's force field shimmered under a tremendous blow, faded, and flared back up. A few more like that and it would fail.

Cy made a fist and launched it toward the larger ship. It hit with tremendous force and sent a shock wave up his arm. Cy laughed. He was a god! Able to reach out and smite evildoers with his mighty right arm! He prepared another fist.

"What the hell was that?" Willer was picking himself up off the deck.

His pilot looked back over her shoulder. Her dope stick waggled when she spoke. "I don't know, Captain. It looked like some kind of green blob. They launched it from the drifter."

Now Willer was on his feet towering over the pilot as he examined her screens. "From the drifter, eh? So it *is* armed. I should've known better than to trust Lando. Well, never mind. Feed 'em a torpedo."

The pilot raised an unplucked eyebrow. "Is that wise? What'll we have then? A half a million tons of scrap, that's what."

Willer pulled his blaster and pressed the barrel against her forehead. "Do what I say or I'll kill you and fly the ship myself!"

The pilot turned back to her board. Next time they hit port she was history. The borg was too weird for her.

Stubby fingers danced over the keys on her control panel. *Hercules* carried a full crew plus a few of Willer's toughs. They manned the secondaries but everything else belonged to her. The pilot selected a launch tube, armed a torpedo, and sent it on its way. "Torpedo fired and running hot."

A green blob slammed into the *Hercules* and pushed it toward a distant asteroid.

Cy used every swear word he'd ever heard. Willer had launched a torpedo! The borg was crazy. So what else was new? Could he stop it? In 6.2 seconds he'd know the answer. Cy held up two of his hands and waited for the missile to hit.

Lando's heart was in his throat as the torpedo made a bright red line across his plot screen and headed straight for the drifter. Cy was using the blobs to hit Willer's ship and the cyborg was trying to stop him!

Two of the green blobs leapt out to intercept the torpedo. There was a brilliant flash of light and the blobs disappeared. And so did all the rest.

Lando checked his vid screens for confirmation. Something was terribly wrong! The greenish light was gone! The drifter was a dark and drifting hulk.

Junk staggered under multiple missile hits. The force field went down. The starboard drive failed. Lights flashed and alarms sounded. Lando wondered if they should scramble into their suits. All things considered it didn't seem worth the trouble.

He touched a button. "All hands to the bridge." It was time to get ready.

Melissa's energy cannon missed the tender but her words went right through her father's heart. Sorenson gave a cry of pain and rage as he realized what he'd done. My God! He'd left his own daughter to die! Blood rushed to his face and Cap felt a terrible sense of shame.

Cap considered suicide, but remembered Willer's words: "He's running away . . . that's what he does best," and realized it was true. If he cared, really cared, he'd *do* something to save his daughter and crew.

But what? What could one man in a tiny spaceship do? All around Cap the asteroids whirled mocking him with their silence. Then he had it. An idea that just might work.

Sorenson's hands were suddenly steady where they touched the controls. He knew what to do, and by God he'd do it!

"Hold your fire." All the ship's weapons fell silent when Willer spoke. *Junk* was helpless and the cyborg wanted to savor the moment. Besides, now that the battle was won, there were mercenary considerations. He had an alien drifter, obviously worth millions, if not billions of credits. Why not add *Junk* to the total? If lots of money was good, more was even better.

Willer turned to his pilot. "Put us alongside. We'll board and neutralize the crew."

The pilot gave a barely perceptible nod and shifted the dope stick from one side of her mouth to the other. Neutralize the crew? Kill little girls? Not her. She'd find a way to avoid the boarding party. She needed time to think. The pilot chose the longest approach she could.

The bombardment had stopped, and without sufficient power for her weapons, *Junk* was forced to do likewise.

Dee looked at the main screen. "They're going to board."

Lando nodded. She was incredibly beautiful. He wanted to say so, to reach out and hold her, but the way Melissa clung to Della's side made that impossible. He pulled his handgun and checked the load instead. "We might as well take a few along with us."

Dee caught his eye. She looked down at Melissa, then back to him. Lando nodded his agreement. At the very last moment one of them would kill her.

Meanwhile Melissa was doing her best to look brave. But it's hard to look brave with tears rolling down your cheeks and a trembling lip. Dee was a comforting presence and Melissa stood as close as she could.

Pik and Della hadn't said anything but Melissa knew anyway. They were about to die. *She* was about to die. It seemed sad, but maybe she'd see Mommy, and that would be good. If only Daddy were here.

Melissa looked up at the view screen and shouted her surprise.

"Pik! Look! It's Daddy!"

Lando took one look, understood Cap's plan, and threw himself at the controls.

"Della! Put every tractor beam we have on *Hercules*! Do the best you can to hold her in place."

Cap grit his teeth. Just a little bit longer, just a little more time, and he'd crush Willer like a bug. He pushed the drive to max.

A proximity alarm went off. Willer couldn't believe his pickups. There was an asteroid headed straight at him!

At first he thought it was a rogue, a buster that had bounced off another roid and tumbled his way.

But a second look told the cyborg he was wrong. The roid was maneuvering to intercept him, and that meant someone was steering it.

Cap! The miserable bastard had poured himself enough manhood to actually do something. The tender! Of course. The crafty old sonovabitch had managed to grab a small asteroid and use it as a battering ram. Well, it wasn't going to work. He yelled at the pilot.

"Full speed ahead! Do it now!"

Not understanding, the pilot took a moment to scan the view screens. All of her attention had been focused on *Junk*. What was Willer screaming about now? Then the pilot saw the asteroid and understood. She shoved the drives to max.

Hercules shivered but that's all. A combination of tractor and pressor beams was holding her in place. Willer screamed and the pilot joined him.

By the time Cap released the asteroid it had lots of inertia. That, plus the fact that Dee was holding *Hercules* in place, equaled maximum effect. The tug was completely destroyed. Both it and the asteroid tumbled away.

There was a long moment of silence on *Junk*'s bridge, followed by a quick radio check on the rest of the crew.

"Cy? Are you there?"

"I sure am, Pik. Is everyone okay?"

"Thanks in part to you," Lando answered. "What you did with those green blobs was absolutely incredible."

"Cap? How 'bout you?"

There was silence for a moment followed by a hoarse croak. "I'm fine, Lando, better than I've been in a long, long time. Melissa? You okay?"

There were tears streaming down Melissa's cheeks, but tears of joy. "I'm fine, Daddy. I'm sorry about what I said. You were wonderful!"

"No," Cap replied, "I wasn't 'wonderful,' but I was better. And maybe that's a first step."

It took three days to check Willer's tug for survivors, there weren't any, and make temporary repairs to all the damage. The good news was that the drifter had somehow started to repair itself. The luminescent green light was back and bit by bit the blobs were reappearing on the surface of its hull.

Cy said, "It's my guess that she'll be as good as new, or old, as the case may be."

The bad news was that *Junk* had sustained even more damage than was immediately apparent. It would be a toss-up to decide whether she was worth the cost of repairs. Still, barring further battles, she'd make it to Pylax. And given the drifter's obvious value, that was far enough. In the meantime however there was a long journey through the asteroids to face.

With the temporary repairs complete, and many days of work ahead, the crew held a party. It centered around the best dinner that Melissa could muster, some nonalcoholic drinks, and the rest of Captain Neubeck's ice cream.

Cap raised his glass. "I wish to propose a toast."

"Hear! Hear!" Lando said, rapping the side of his glass with a spoon.

Cap smiled. "To the chef, my beautiful daughter Melissa, the most important person in my life!"

Melissa beamed happily, and raised her glass. "To Daddy, and a ship named *Junk*!" Everyone laughed.

Cy waited until the laughter died down to raise his glass, a symbolic gesture since he couldn't drink from it, but appropriate nonetheless.

"And my toast is to 'them,' the ones who built the drifter, and disappeared. Sol bless them wherever they are . . . and thanks for the ship!"

That brought more laughter. Now it was Dee's turn. Her eyes sparkled as they swept the table and stopped on Lando. "My toast is to all of you, for accepting me into your family, and for giving me something a bounty can't buy!"

Lando smiled and raised his glass high. "And I give you my father's favorite toast. 'To the end of this run, and the start of another!' "

Outside, beyond *Junk*'s durasteel hull, the asteroids and stars continued to dance. They knew what lay ahead but wouldn't tell.

The Author

William C. Dietz lives with his wife, daughters, cats, and hamsters in Seattle where he does PR work for a large corporation. Over the years Dietz has worked as a surgical technician, a news writer, a television producer-director, a college instructor, and other things he'd rather forget.

DAVID DRAKE

__NORTHWORLD 0-441-84830-3/$3.95

The consensus ruled twelve hundred worlds—but not Northworld.
Three fleets had been dispatched to probe the enigma of Northworld. None returned. Now, Commissioner Nils Hansen must
face the challenge of the distant planet. There he will confront a
world at war, a world of androids...all unique, all lethal.

__SURFACE ACTION 0-441-36375-X/$4.50

Venus has been transformed into a world of underwater habitats
for Earth's survivors. Battles on Venus must be fought on the
ocean's exotic surface. Johnnie Gordon trained his entire life for
battle, and now his time has come to live a warrior's life on the
high seas.

THE FLEET Edited by David Drake and Bill Fawcett

The soldiers of the Human/Alien Alliance come from different
worlds and different cultures. But they share a common mission:
to reclaim occupied space from the savage Khalian invaders.

__BREAKTHROUGH   0-441-24105-0/$3.95
__COUNTERATTACK   0-441-24104-2/$3.95
__SWORN ALLIES   0-441-24090-9/$3.95